Found Wanting

By

JJ Lambert

Black Bee Books Ltd.

First Published in Great Britain in 2024 by
Black Bee Books Ltd
Bryn Heulog, Talley
Llandeilo, Wales SA19 7YH
Copyright © JJ Lambert 2024

Cover Image © katelouisepowell.com
Cover Design © Huw Francis

ISBN: (Paperback) 978-1-913853-12-9
ISBN: (eBook) 978-1-913853-13-6

www.blackbeebooks.wales

Acknowledgements

Many people have read and offered opinions on this novel or its subjects and I am grateful to them all. I would like to say a particular thank you to Sue Cook, Wendy Davies, Jeremy Dixon, Conway Emmett, Annabelle Lambert, Jon/Fine Stargardt, Grace Quantock, WAB, Rin Woolley and to the exquisitely talented and golden-hearted Janna Miller. Thanks too to Vicky Macdougall and Eleanor Macdougall for their support.

I have spent nearly twenty years as part of the home educating community, and it's been a joy to have witnessed so many children grow up into thriving, interesting adults. Spending time with so many different families was a privilege and I am especially grateful to everyone who allowed me to practice my playwriting and directing 'skills' on them.

I am also grateful to the Queer community of Wales for existing, in all its manifestations, and acknowledge their courage in facing appalling, uniformed bigotry and prejudice as they lead their lives.

Angharad

I live in Wales. In the middle. The bit where nobody goes on holiday.

Llanyfenni would be a small town if it was in England, but in Wales the small towns are more important. We have a Starbucks now, but it's out on the main road. People got really excited about the Starbucks, as if it was an umbilical cord to London and Seattle, like our town was chosen as worthy. But I think if that was the case the Starbucks would be in town and you wouldn't have to run across the by-pass to get to it.

I've been home educated all my life. My mum says that isn't the same as home-schooled. There are probably more of us around than you realise. Like rats. In a good way – rats are cute. I've never been to school because my mum worried that school would make me learn about fossils and evidence-based theories. We didn't need evidence, because we had faith. Well, I wanted to have faith, but the whole religion thing was something I was trying not to think about too much.

We went to church every Sunday. There were no other girls my age there. There was a boy – Sam. He was sixteen. We used to be in Sunday School together, but then I figured that no one would care if we skipped it as long as we didn't make a big deal out of it. It was much nicer in the graveyard. Unless it was raining, which it does a lot in Wales. When it rained, we sat under the lychgate, opposite each other on the old stone benches and looked at our phones. None of the adults ever said anything about it.

I met Faith on the first Sunday in May, when she came to our church. It was sunny, and really hot outside. Everyone kept telling each other to make the most of it because it wouldn't last. I was wearing my summer dress, obediently making the best of it, even though I knew it would be cold inside. It's always cold inside. A few years ago, we talked about getting big electric heaters, but in the end Mr Thomas decided that we didn't want to end up on the slippery slope to becoming addicted to luxury like a Catholic.

That morning, I was focussed on trying to avoid Cerys, who for some old-lady reason had decided ages ago that we had a special bond. Obviously this wasn't true, because I am fifteen and she is old, so I mainly listened while she told me about going to the garden centre with her friend Sue, or a hedgehog that she'd seen, or what her neighbour thought about the new bus times. I know it's important to be respectful to old people, and I usually am, but that Sunday it just felt too hot.

Faith walked in to the church beside her mum like she knew everyone was watching her and she liked it. She was wearing a red dress that was way too short. I thought maybe her family didn't have much money and she had grown out of the dress a bit but they couldn't afford a new one. I didn't stare, even though she was the most beautiful person I had ever seen in real life. I just smiled, polite and friendly. That's what we do, in our church.

My mum headed straight for them, hissing at me to follow her. 'Hi,' she said, loudly and clearly.

Even though my mum is actually English and only moved here twenty years ago, she likes to pretend she's Welsh and making a special effort to be understood by incomers. It was obvious Faith and her Mum were incomers. They introduced themselves, and us, and then kept on smiling at each other. Like we were toddlers and they were about to organise a playdate. I might not be the most socially aware teenager, but even I could tell that Faith probably wasn't the playdate type. Her mum was chatting away in an English accent. Faith didn't say anything at all. She wasn't smiling, or being polite and friendly. She looked more like she might just storm out and set fire to something. I wished I had shaved my legs.

Our mums sat down together, and then my dad, so Faith and I were left on the end. There was a space between us, the longest it could be without me falling off. Even from there, she smelt like strawberries. The whole way through the first reading I sat still and looked forward. I was trying to be a good example. But I could hardly understand what Mr Thomas was saying. I kept wondering why she was here. She was obviously far too cool to be religious.

After the second hymn, when the Sunday School go out, Sam stood up as if this was like any other Sunday. I couldn't let him go alone, so I followed him. And Faith followed me. I could feel her behind me, all the way down the nave. Tried to remember how I normally walked.

Sam lifted the big old latch and pulled the door back slowly. We are pretty good at this now. The sun made me blink after the dark church. I followed Sam out into the porch. He stopped, suddenly, and turned around, as if he had noticed something was different. We all stood, awkwardly. Sam started to smile, polite and friendly. I hoped my smile had looked a bit less rigid; he looked like a corpse.

I waited for someone to speak. I wondered who it would be. Not Sam, I guessed, and probably not me. 'So.' Faith said, looking around.

She sounded pretty judgemental. I kept smiling. 'Have you been in Llanyfenni long?' I asked her, realising halfway through that I was accidentally using the special voice my mum uses to our window cleaner.

Faith looked at me, like she was laughing a bit inside. 'Not long,' she said. 'Everyone said it would be a shit-hole, but I like it.'

I tried not to look alarmed. I knew in theory that teenagers said things like that, they just weren't usually talking to me. And then, after the alarm, I felt a bit cross on Llanyfenni's behalf. 'Where do you come from?' I tried not to sound aggressive.

'Worcester. Big city. Lots of shops, that kind of thing. A train that comes more than twice a day.'

Her eyes still looked like she might still be laughing. At me, I guessed. Or Llanyfenni. My head felt prickly. Sam had wandered away, and was sitting against the wall, as if he wasn't interested in what Faith thought. 'We don't do much out here,' I said. 'Just sit. Sometimes there's butterflies.'

I was embarrassed, in case she thought it was weird, sitting out here with Sam and staring at the flowers. Then I felt disloyal to Sam for thinking it. Faith smiled, finally. 'Have I made it awkward? I'm sorry. Sometimes I'm a bit of a dick. I'm just nervous.'

Relief flooded through me. I realised I was smiling back, a real smile. I shook my head. 'It's fine.'

We sat down next to Sam, one on each side. I hoped he was okay. Sam didn't generally seem to like being close to people, and now he was sandwiched in on both sides. I decided not to worry about him. He'd have to take care of himself for now.

The wall of the church was warm from the sun. I felt myself relax against it. 'Mum wanted to come to church straight away to get to know people,' Faith said.

I looked across at her. Her head was tipped back against the wall, but I was sure her eyes were open. 'There's not many people to get to know. Not our age anyway. No boys,' I said, as if I thought she had been assuming there were a load of gorgeous boys hiding behind a pillar.

She wrinkled her face up. 'That's okay. I'm not that invested in meeting people. I'm always meeting people. That's the easy bit. It's trying to get rid of them that's hard, don't you think?'

She turned her head and looked across Sam, at me. I tried to look non-committal, like I also had that problem. 'Anyway,' she smiled again, 'I've met you two.'

And she lay back against the warm hard wall of the church

and closed her eyes and eventually so did I, and no one spoke. I felt the sun warming me up all the way through and when I opened them Faith was gone and it was the end of church and everyone was coming out and blinking in the light and chatting and laughing and it was time to walk home for lunch.

Faith came to church every week in May. We always sat together and every week the sun was shining and Sam stood up when it was Sunday School time and we followed him out. I never got around to asking Sam if he minded Faith coming with us, maybe because Sam and I never had that kind of friendship. It wasn't even really friendship, just sitting together not talking. Every week Faith wore the same too-short dress, and I made sure I didn't stare, or even look, at her long brown legs. I wasn't sure if Sam was having the same problem.

After church, we'd walk round to the front and Faith's mum would be chatting to my mum, or to one of the old people. When she saw Faith, Faith's mum would smile a huge relieved smile, as if Faith was the loveliest thing she could possibly imagine seeing, finish her conversation and they'd go off together.

Apart from church, I didn't really go out. That was another thing I liked about Sam. I knew he spent hours in his room, on his computer. He would never ask questions about what I did all day, or act like I should be different. I was pretty sure it wasn't weird not to go out. There was no reason to be ashamed. I was, anyway.

I do, usually, like being with my parents. They never seem to think I should be out, vaping and laughing with other girls. My dad is a policeman, but round here that's mainly going to people's houses when they've had their quad bike stolen and writing down the details. They never seem to get the bikes back. You see kids riding around on them. My dad never looks that worried. Mainly my dad likes going along to the youth club and playing football with the kids. He says that's community relations. He also likes helping old ladies find their cats, and telling them about day centres and lunch clubs. And making sure the man that sleeps in the bus stop has a cup of coffee in the mornings. That kind of thing. I love him, but I'm not sure that he's a very good policeman. Whenever you see riots on the news, he always nods wisely, as if the reason we don't have riots in Llanyfenni is because of all the football and cat finding. When he's at home we play chess. I'm pretty good against him, but it's not like there's anyone else who wants to play me. When we were all younger, the other home ed kids and I used to play all the time, but now they are busy dying their hair and sitting round on walls showing their cleavage and pretending to ignore the boys. I'm pretty sure they want to forget the afternoons they spent trying to beat me. And failing, because they never bothered to learn any of the openings and kept forgetting to castle.

My mum works now that I'm older, so theoretically I'm educating myself. That's called autonomous education and will teach me self-motivation and resilience. I mainly scroll through Instagram, feel a bit depressed, and play computer games. I'm pretty good at the games because I've nothing else to do so I can just keep practising till I get it. Though something on Twitter said the games have algorithms in them that means they get easier if you keep playing so you feel like you're making progress even if you're shit. So the baddies get worse at shooting each time, and you have have to be less accurate, that kind of thing. Taking this into account, it's possible that I'm actually shit. I'm supposed to do stuff every day on a couple of websites – maths and physics and English. Sometimes I do.

My mum says home educated teens are like chrysalises, who need space and time to discover who they really are and that they suddenly come out of their bedrooms and are beautiful butterflies. I have literally no idea what she's basing this on – the other girls round here have been butterflies all along. I just didn't realise that was what we were aiming at. It's like everyone changed the rules suddenly and being good at chess and polite got less important than having boobs and wearing as little as possible, and pretending to think boys are hilarious and clever, even when they aren't. Especially when they aren't.

Anyway, I guess basically, before Faith, I wasn't really doing much. So sitting against a church wall was the social highlight of my week. I'd have felt better about that if I'd known that that bit of my life was pretty much over.

Brad

Am lonely. So fucking lonely.

Angharad

I was relieved when Faith turned up wearing brand new Vans on the first Sunday of June. Still wearing the very short dress but by then I couldn't picture her in a normal dress. Even when I thought about the winter, in my imagination she was lolling against the church wall bundled up in a huge coat with her tiny red dress underneath. Or marching to church through a snowstorm in her tiny red dress, snowflakes in her hair. In my imagination, she was warm, even though her dress was too short.

I didn't want to think of her as having a mum who didn't care or was too poor to buy her clothes. Once I saw the Vans I knew they must be okay really. No-one would waste money on Vans if they didn't have enough money for proper clothes. I wished that she'd wear something more sensible though. I saw the way that Mr. Thomas looked at her.

But the next Sunday, Faith wasn't there. Her mum came, and stood very close to Cerys and Sue, but she wasn't saying much. As if something bad had happened and she was putting a brave face on it. I didn't ask about Faith. I didn't want to act like I thought we were friends. I thought Faith probably had other, real friends. I couldn't imagine, say, Faith and I going shopping together, or for a walk.

But it turned out I was wrong. Faith was waiting for me after church. 'I know it's crap and dull and for old men, but do you want to go to that thing in the park? The steam engines and that? Everything's shit.'

That seemed a bit dramatic, but I was flattered she'd asked. 'Do you need to tell your mum?' I asked, and she stared at me.

'Do you?'

'No,' I said.

We wandered off towards the park. The show was cool, really, even if I rolled my eyes whenever Mum suggested we should go. It happened every year and there were kiddie fairground rides and ice cream vans and dog display teams as well as the old men standing around staring at massive machines and nodding wisely with a can of beer in their hand. Occasionally something would let out a load of steam and a loud whistle that you could hear across the whole town. I secretly loved steam tractors, and the smell of the hot oil and especially the bit where they all drove round in a big circle at the same time at the end of the day. I hoped I wouldn't get excited in front of Faith.

We had to pay to get in, but Faith said she'd pay for both of us. I was relieved because I never had much money and I wanted to be able to buy her an ice cream later on. In the corner of the playing fields there was a sort of hill with a few trees and then the wall, with the road and houses behind. There was a stone circle, but not an old one, just a modern one made to look old. In the main field there were all the tents and marquees and open air stands.

You could buy loads of different random things: tiny spanners and huge spanners and old car mirrors, geraniums or cucumber plants or hot dogs or photos of Llanyfenni in the old days. There was a place where you could hold an owl and a place where you could watch someone making animals out of wood with a chainsaw, all that kind of stuff. We wandered through them. Some of the old men nodded at me because they knew my parents, which was embarrassing.

There was a big show area in the middle, the usual thing, with those metal barriers around it. We leaned on the barriers. They were hot, almost burning, but I kept my arm there, as if the pain would keep me focussed. Faith's elbow was touching mine. She had a nice elbow. Our elbows looked cute together.

There were stunt motorbike riders in the middle of the showground, doing their thing. They were run by a guy in the town – Dai Morgan – but they travelled all over, getting paid for it too.

They were pretty good. One of them especially. He had that long and lean relaxed sort of look, like he could do this sort of thing all day. Leaping through burning hoops and jumping off ramps. There was loud music thumping through the speakers, nearly drowning out the steam whistles. At the end he rode once round, fast, skidding round the corners while everyone clapped and cheered. He finished by the entrance and took off his helmet.

I wasn't surprised to see he had long shaggy blond hair, it seemed exactly the right sort of hair for a stunt man. A girl in jeans and hardly any top ran across to him, boobs bouncing everywhere. She put her arms round him like he was the most amazing thing she'd ever seen. He held the bike with one hand and sort of picked her up with the other and she wrapped her legs around him squealing for a second. I felt uncomfortable watching them. I didn't want to look at Faith in case she'd seen me staring. She obviously had though. She rolled her eyes and snorted. 'Do you know them?'

I felt like I should, when I'd lived here all my life, but they weren't exactly the sort of people I met. I shook my head. Faith didn't bother to lower her voice. 'That's Ella, she goes to my dance group.'

'Oh.'

'And his name's Jake. Of course,' she giggled and I did too, because of course that's exactly the kind of name someone like that would have.

'How old is he?'

'I don't know… Twenty-one?'

'Are they going out?'

I did my best not to sound disapproving. I couldn't imagine someone my age going out with someone like Jake. 'She wishes,' Faith sounded dismissive. 'She thinks if she sucks him off enough it's love. He's a mechanic at the garage down the road from mine and she's always hanging around down there. Rubbing her hand up and down coke bottles and licking lollipops, that kind of thing.'

I was glad I wasn't looking at her. I was pretty sure I liked Faith, but it shocked me when she spoke like that. It made me feel like I was being a teenager wrong. I couldn't imagine myself ever saying something like that. I practised quickly, in my head. Even in my imagination I couldn't say it right. I felt a bit sad. I had thought that being here, with a friend, meant I was finally getting normal, but there was obviously more to work on. I sighed. Faith looked at me, smiling. 'What?'

I smiled back. 'Nothing. Do you want to go get an ice cream?'

'And a burger? I'll treat you,'

'Do you have a job?'

She shrugged. 'Sort of. I do some stuff for a friend. You know.'

I nodded. I didn't know. We wandered to the ice cream van and then ate ice creams while we queued for the burger van. I tried to keep my eyes on the person in front of me, so no old people came up to tell me about their old people stuff in front of Faith. Faith was quiet. Maybe feeling guilty about being judgemental, but I suspected not. I had never, in my life, heard anyone say the sorts of things that Faith said without even blushing.

We ate the burgers and chips as we walked round. I showed Faith the sheep and tried to remember what all the different breeds were. Faith showed me the stage where she was supposed to be dancing later. I wondered if she wanted me to watch her. I still couldn't imagine Faith at a dance class, with people like Ella. When I told her that, she laughed. 'I get paid. I help out. I'm good, better than anyone here.' She glanced at me. 'No offence.'

I shrugged. I wasn't offended. I liked the idea of Faith

telling that girl what to do. When we'd finished eating, she put the cartons in the bin. I was trying not to keep adding and subtracting marks for how Faith behaved, because I knew that was definitely weird and not okay, but it was a relief to be adding some marks for her not littering.

There was a chirrup and Faith reached into her bag and pulled out her phone. It was nicer than I'd expect a poor person to have. She saw me looking at it and laughed a bit at my expression. 'It's only an old one.'

It didn't look like an old phone. But then I'm not a phone expert. She read the message. 'Fuck,' she said and put her phone back in her bag. I wasn't sure if she was angry.

It didn't seem weird when she took my hand. Her hands were soft, and warm from the sun, and greasy from the burger and the chips. I wasn't sure if I'd held a girl's hand before. Not since playgroup. It felt brave, touching someone, being touched. But nice too, like we were a team now.

She led the way through the tents and caravans and up the hill. There were a few groups of people up there, the field spread out below. Faith took me to the oak and sat down, pulling me with her. 'Thank you,' she said, looking at me properly, 'For coming with me.'

'Are you okay?'

Her head tilted a bit 'Why?'

I didn't want to annoy her by asking about the text, or reminding her that earlier she had said everything was shit. Faith looked at me as if she was laughing at me again, but kindly. 'I'm not sure. But I can't tell you about it or you'll think I'm not very nice.'

It seemed a bit mean to tell her that I had never thought she was a nice person. I was also pretty sure that if you were beautiful and went to school and taught dance groups and had a cute phone and new cool shoes that life really couldn't possibly be that hard. It seemed rude to say that. She smiled at me again. 'I'm trying though, I really am. It's like a fresh start for me, coming here. For mum too.'

I wondered vaguely why anyone would need a fresh start. I leaned back on the tree, feeling the ridges of the trunk against my spine. I tipped my head back and closed my eyes. I could smell candyfloss. Even up here, you could hear the steam engines chugging away and smell the smoke.

'You know this isn't normal? This place?' Faith's voice sounded like she was smiling.

I kept my eyes closed. I breathed in a whole lungful of candy floss smell. We were still holding hands. Faith's hand was warm and sweaty. I felt like I was swimming in sunlight.

'What's Worcester like, then?'

'It's like the real world. You know, normal people. Doing normal stuff.'

'No steam tractors?'

She laughed and I let go of her hand and opened my eyes to look at her.

*

She kissed me. Or maybe I kissed her. Her lips still had salt on from the chips and her mouth tasted like burger. She had put her hands on my cheeks, holding my face. I stopped and looked at her, into her huge blue eyes. No one had ever touched me like that before. I panicked; this was way out of my league. I'd be doing it wrong and she'd laugh at me. Then we were kissing again, and I stopped worrying, there wasn't space in my brain. My whole body was fizzing. I realised I was smiling.

When the kissing stopped, I looked around, suddenly worried about who was watching us, and relieved that no one seemed to be. I turned back to Faith, who was already on her feet. 'Don't freak out, Angharad. I'll go.'

She still said my name wrong. English people usually do.

She ran off across the grass, down the hill. I watched her until she disappeared into the groups of people milling around.

Faith

I knew I'd screwed up as soon as I was halfway across the field. It wasn't Angharad's fault she freaked out. She's probably never even looked at a girl before, let alone kissed one. I should have handled it better, apologised maybe. I wasn't really sure how apologising worked, but I was familiar with the theory.

When I first saw Angharad, all prim and proper in her embarrassing dress and weird sandals, smiling hard, I was worried I would accidentally get involved. I don't mean to fancy people who'll reject me, it just happens. And if I'd imagined the person least likely to like me back, it'd be Angharad.

I walked back through the blokes waving owls around and the kids waving ice creams. Hoped that I didn't see Jake or Ella. I wasn't in the mood for either of them.

People were smiling at me as I passed, not just men staring at my legs but all sorts of people. Friendly people. In Llanyfenni, there's a lot of friendly people. Very friendly. Always asking questions, really personal questions, not holding back. You'd get used to it, I guessed. Even in church, where you'd think people would have more important things to think about there were endless questions. Not from Angharad though. She didn't really seem to talk at all. Maybe that was my new type. Silent and religious. Like a nun.

Church really wasn't my sort of place, historically. But it looked like you'd imagine, long wooden seats and stained glass that the light shone through. It seemed best not to think about how this had turned into the nicest part of the week now, and it was definitely not something I was going to tell anyone. Seeing Angharad, head tipped back against the church, eyes closed and saying nothing was definitely worth a bit of god stuff and some old people looking at me as if I was the literal devil. Probably the red dress didn't help.

But there was just something lovely about Angharad. Something pure, even though she was obviously completely brainwashed by all the church stuff. I kept reminding myself I hardly knew her. Tried not to think about her, like that. Kept finding myself thinking about her, like that. Stopping myself. Imagining her saying things in her funny accent. Imagining my hands on her pale, soft shoulders. When I held them, her hands were so soft. I should have known I'd screw it up.

And then there was Jed. Not so exciting, not so hot. Still distracting. Poor, posh, sweaty Jed. If he hadn't been texting me like the world was about to end and it was my fault, I'd probably have kept it together and not come on to Angharad. Or let her come on to me. Whichever. I wasn't sure what was going on with Jed, but he was making a lot of fuss about it. I should probably check in, but it was hard to imagine what could possibly be that bad.

I couldn't find Mum when I got in. It was a bit cooler in the house, and I really wanted to just lie down in the dark and have a think. But I knew if I didn't go and find her I'd just fret. It would probably end up being less hassle to fetch her home. I was standing in the middle of the room, psyching myself to go back out in the heat when Phil rang. It was obviously my day to be dealing with stressed out Worcester boys. 'Just wondering how it's going?'

'Why?'

He sighed. 'Don't be prickly, Faith.'

I could be prickly if I wanted, so I ignored that and waited to find out what he actually wanted. 'Business going okay?'

I didn't want to think about mine and Phil's 'business'. 'Fine.'

'How's your mum?'

'Okay. Not great.'

More silence. This wasn't how things usually were between me and Phil. I felt like I might cry. Maybe I had some weird heatstroke. Or was allergic to steam tractors. I sighed. 'Pretty shit, actually.'

Phil sighed too. 'Come up. I need to talk to you anyway. Come and stay with us for a bit.'

Like we were the kind of people who invited each other to stay, instead of the kind who got pissed together and fell asleep on the floor. Like he worked in an estate agents or a bank, not like some low-key stoner in a grungy flat. So alarm bells should have been ringing.

But I was a pillock, and anyway, I liked Phil. I told him I'd think about it, grabbed my sunglasses and headed out the door to track down my mum.

It was still hot. I didn't mind it though. Everyone said Wales would just be rain and sheep, so I'm still happy every day when the sun comes up and it's another cloudless blue sky. And Llanyfenni is gorgeous in the sunshine, with little white flowers growing beside the road and big fat bees coming up to you as if they think you might be a flower. People don't generally think I might be a flower.

I walked in the shade, breathing deeply and feeling the heat filling my lungs. Everything was obviously still shit, but at least it wasn't shit and raining. And even the sheep were pretty cute. It still made me laugh, when you could hear them all baa-ing for their lambs in the evenings, or when you saw them going past in lorries with their noses poking out. Off to be killed and made into chops, which were also a good thing, except not for the lambs.

It was nice walking around, sun on my face, red kites going round in circles like they just couldn't be bothered, whistling away. Nice if I didn't think of all the things Mum might be up to. I headed towards the church, just because I had to be heading somewhere and definitely not in case Angharad was walking home that way.

When I got there, Cerys was just locking up. I guessed some weird Sunday night church thing had been on. There were loads of those, all times of day. Every week that old grouch Andrew Thomas listed them. Meals and prayers and choir practise and slide shows about old people building churches in random parts of Africa like they were saviours. A whole social life for people that had to make friends without drugs, alcohol or cigarettes. I could see how Angharad fit right in.

Since Cerys is the kind of old biddy that knows everything about everybody, I figured she might know where Mum was. She had Sue with her, another smiling old biddy. I was optimistic. Between the two gossipy old biddies, surely one of them would have seen her. She might even have been at the slide show or meal or whatever. Anything is possible with my Mum.

I was heading towards the church gate, watching them. And when the door was locked, Cerys passed the key across to Sue, and for a moment they stood still, smiling at each other. Nothing else, but there was something about it that made me stop. They might not have been snogging or fingering each other, but after a second, I turned and walked away. I was probably wrong. Smiling into each other's eyes wasn't any kind of evidence of anything.

I sighed to myself. If lesbians were a bit more visible in Llanyfenni, you wouldn't have to go around eyeing up random old ladies like a weirdo. Maybe Sunday night was LGBTQ night at church and Cerys and Sue had been going along quietly for forty years, and now true love had blossomed. Maybe they would be the queer family I was supposed to have at some point. Me and Cerys and Sue. Sue had quite a beard, but probably Cerys was nice enough to see beyond that, and I could try to be.

I felt a bit cheerier as I walked away. If there was hope for Cerys and Sue, there was probably hope for me.

I found my Mum around the corner. I had no idea why she would be there. I wondered if she had been watching Cerys and Sue too. Maybe watching old ladies like a sicko ran in my genes. I was worried enough about the other stuff that might run in my genes without that. It didn't seem fair that other people got being musical and good at maths in their genes and I had craving vodka, insomnia and falling for the wrong people.

I didn't ask Mum why she was just standing there. I didn't tell her that I'd been worried when she wasn't home. Just pretended I was heading home myself, and told her there was beer in the fridge and that I'd buy us chips on the way. She stared at me suspiciously for a minute, but I'm pretty convincing and beer and chips is always a safe bet. In the end she nodded, and we headed for the chippy.

She fell asleep halfway through her beer. I watched her head slowly tipping forwards, dribble sliding down her chin. Phoned Jess and told her that I wouldn't be dancing, my mum was ill. Could hear her sighing. Without me, the dance show didn't exactly have much. 'I bet Ella could do my dance,' I said.

She sighed again. I put a blanket over my mum. I loved her and I was sick of her. Then I called Phil and said I'd see him on Monday. I'd go back in a few days, when I could face it all. I carefully didn't let myself think about what my mum would do without me.

Angharad

Faith wasn't at church the next week. I wasn't that surprised, I was relieved. I wouldn't have known what to say. Even thinking about her made me blush. I tested it in the mirror, whispering her name, and watching my cheeks turn red.

I missed her when we sat outside though.

Her mum still looked like she was being brave and strong while life threw problem after problem at her. After church, I hung around for a few minutes in case she looked like she wanted to give me a message from Faith, but she headed off, Cerys holding onto her arm. I thought it was nice of Faith's mum to be so kind to poor, old, boring Cerys.

I saw Ella on Friday, in the street, outside Boots, which for some reason is the cool spot to hang out round here. She was standing with one leg stretched out, up on the railing, with a couple of boys I didn't know watching her admiringly. Which pretty much summed her up. I was nervous about talking to her, but then remembered how rude Faith had been about her and felt a bit sorry for her instead. 'Ella.'

She raised her eyebrows, with a bit of a sneer. I stopped feeling sorry for her.

'Have you seen Faith? Since Sunday?'

Her forehead wrinkled, she looked all sour. 'That slut?'

'Is she?'

It was one of the things I'd been wondering. I'd been meaning to have a proper think about Faith and the kiss and stuff, but it had been easier not to. Sometimes magazines make it sound like snogging your girl friends is just a normal part of being a teenager, practising for when you get a boyfriend. Though I couldn't imagine Faith needed much practise, she had seemed very good at it to me. I just wanted to know what it had meant, for her.

Ella's face got even sourer. 'She's gone up north with that

Jake,' she looked me up and down, 'The bike guy. My bike guy. Pathetic'

'Are you sure?'

'She's had a thing for him since she got here. She's desperate.'

I walked away. My eyes felt stingy. What had I expected? I asked myself furiously.

By the next Sunday, I was nervous all over again about seeing Faith. And a bit cross. Girls who came to church weren't also supposed to be going off for weekends with boys. Men. I wasn't sure how old Jake was, but he definitely wasn't fifteen. Or even sixteen. If he really was twenty-one, I was sure that made him a man. 'I don't know where Faith is,' I said casually to Sam.

He looked carefully at the ground and didn't reply. I wondered if someone had said something about us, kissing. In Llanyfenni, gossip gets more and more exciting the more people that get involved. With my luck, I'd be forty and still hearing about the time I was naked in the park with some girl. Possibly driving a steam engine. I carried on quickly, before that thought could get any further. 'Have you seen her?'

He took a while to answer. 'No,'

So that was that. Maybe she had realised she shouldn't really be coming to church if she wasn't even trying to believe and behave properly. Maybe her mum had told her to stay home until she was ready to be a proper Christian. I realised the voice in my head was being a bit of a sanctimonious cow. Religion is sneaky like that, I think. You think you are having an opinion and then realise it's someone else's opinion, possibly someone two thousand years ago, and it's probably crap.

I watched out for Faith's mum afterwards. It looked like the church women had taken her under their wings. I knew that if she was having a difficult time they would be offering prayers, and food and cups of tea. In the past, we've even raised money to help people who needed it. I noticed that even though they still sat next to her in church, my parents didn't seem to be in the group of helpful people.

I was half expecting them to mention Faith not being there on the way home but they were busy discussing how humid it was, and whether Sue praying for rain for the garden was really godly. My Dad, obviously, thought that she was probably doing it for everyone's benefit, and that it was a good use of prayer, and my Mum rolled her eyes and tutted, which means that she thinks my Dad is a naïve fool.

On Monday, I saw Jake in town. In the pedestrianised bit. I was partly hanging around in town to see if Faith turned up, but I was also going to the library. I didn't go that often, but I was a member, and I thought there might be some kind of useful book. I knew 'How to feel when you kiss a girl who runs away' was too much to hope for, and I had read all the YA a long time ago, but I figured it was worth a try.

When I saw Jake, I was about to pretend I didn't know who he was and just keep walking, looking thoughtful, but he caught my eye and then headed across towards me. I stopped. He was very tall, and had stubble. Proper stubble, like an adult. I couldn't believe what Faith and Ella said about each other. I couldn't imagine anything more alarming than being anywhere near his underwear, let alone what was underneath it. I could feel my chest getting tight. Just breathe, I told myself. He stopped square in front of me. 'Are you Faith's friend? Ella said you were.'

'Well…'

He looked a bit irritated so I carried on, feeling my voice getting high. 'I don't really know. I like her, and I thought maybe she liked me, and we did go to the vintage thing together –'

I realised he'd been there and what he'd been doing and felt myself blushing '– so I kind of thought we might be friends. But I don't know.'

'Come and have a coffee?'

I guess I looked pretty terrified, because that's how I felt and he said 'Only over there,' – pointing at Caffi Sosban – 'please.'

He had massive brown eyes. Caffi Sosban was where all the old people hung out in the week and they sold tea in a mug for 99p and an all day breakfast for £4, it didn't seem like the kind of place anyone would expect you to touch their penis. Plus, I quite liked the idea of someone walking past and seeing me with Jake. Especially Ella. Or the bitchy home ed girls. Even Cerys. Seeing me sitting with a hot boy in a town might show her that I really wasn't that interested in her hedgehog stories because I was a different, much cooler, sort of teenager than she thought. So I walked in with him.

The café was full of babies and pushchairs and men sitting and staring glumly out looking as if they still hadn't got used to not being allowed to smoke. There was a bit of awkwardness when I tried to aim for a table by the window and then realised that Jake, just as firmly, was heading for a table all alone further back. We obviously had different goals about public visibility. I gave in and followed him.

We sat across the red checked table cloth from each other and I wished it was a bit cleaner. If this was the only hour of my life I was going to spend sitting with a gorgeous man in a leather jacket, I'd have liked it if it wasn't so crumby. And ketchupy.

Jake called across for coffee. I had started drinking coffee a few months ago and hopefully would just drink it casually without making weird expressions.

'So,' he said, looking serious 'You're Angharad, right? I've seen you around.'

I nodded. Wow, he was so beautiful. No wonder Faith had gone off without a backwards glance. I realised I probably would too. I tried to look attentive. And relaxed. I hoped that I wouldn't faint.

'Did you have a nice time, at the weekend?' I asked politely.

He looked confused. Even his eyebrows were sexy. 'With Faith?' I explained

'I wasn't with Faith. I was doing a show. Up north. Llandudno.' He smiled cheerfully. 'It was good. But then I came back and got a mouthful from Ella,' I tried to ignore the image in my head, 'and it turns out Faith's disappeared. Dunno why Ella thought Faith would be with me, she just freaked out.'

He shrugged as if girls freaking out was just something that happened, like the weather. I opened my mouth, but wasn't sure what to say. Jake nodded at me, 'I know, weird. And it turns out Faith didn't do some show thing she was supposed to do with Ella, no biggie, but then she didn't turn up at dance the next week.'

The waitress brought two coffees over. Jake winked at her and poured sugar into both mugs. When he handed one to me, our fingers touched. He kept talking. 'So I went round to her's on Thursday and she wasn't there and her mum was in a right state, and I guess no one's seen her since?'

I shook my head. It was too much to take in. I hadn't realised Faith was so popular. 'I didn't know you were friends,' I said, feeling like a sulky toddler left out a party and trying not to.

He looked a bit blank. 'Well. I thought she must have gone to Worcester, but she never said, and she's usually only gone a day or two. And she's not answering her phone.'

I didn't even have her phone number. She'd just run off. I felt like I needed to sort out some facts. I tried to sound casual. 'So you two are seeing each other?'

'What?' he looked confused, and I blushed again, even though I didn't know what I was embarrassed about yet. 'For fucks sake, Angharad. This isn't some school kid drama. She sells me weed.' He looked properly incredulous I might not have realised this, as if I was the only person in town not queueing up at Faith's house to buy drugs.

I thought I might cry. I looked carefully at the table. 'Angharad, I thought you knew. I mean, everyone knows. It's not some big secret.' I wasn't sure how that was supposed to make me feel any better.

Jake shrugged. 'But the thing is, she hasn't come back.'

He reached across the table and took my hand. I kept looking down. The skin on his hand was hard and his hand was huge, and wrapped all around mine. Like a leather glove, keeping my hand safe.

His chair scraped on the floor as he stood up and came around beside me, so I was between him and the wall. I could feel him looking at me. He put his arm around me, and I knew I was really going to cry, like a kid. I felt pathetic. I could feel snot edging it's way down from my nose. He smelt like leather and oil, and tobacco. I could feel his muscles through my shirt.

He handed me a serviette. I wiped my nose quickly. 'Jeez, Angharad, now that's twice this week I've had a girl crying on me in here.'

He didn't sound that worried though. I was cross at the idea that people might think I was another girl crying over him. I wasn't actually that sure why I was crying. I sat up and tried to stop. 'I was hoping you knew where she was,' he grinned at me, 'But I guess you're as clueless as the rest of us.'

He swallowed his coffee. 'Right, okay, I better shoot off.'

'Bye, then,'

He looked into my eyes, as if he was properly looking at me. And I wasn't crying any more. He grinned at me, and stood up. 'You're pretty cute when you smile.'

'It's been nice to meet you,'

'Sure, Angharad, it's been smashing.'

And he turned and loped off, just letting the door swing shut behind him. The waitress looked at me pityingly. 'Shut your mouth, cariad, you'll catch flies.'

Faith

I didn't take much stuff to Worcester. Wore my new trainers. I might be feeling pathetic, but I don't ever want to look it.

I got the train. That's pretty much the only option. The buses only go to Brecon, and I have no idea why anyone would want to go to Brecon. The train is nice, trundling along up the mountains and sometimes stopping at platforms in the middle of nowhere to let off people with hiking boots and waterproofs and holding maps.

I hadn't been to Phil's new house before. He'd moved to Broadway a few weeks before. He was all pleased with himself for moving, but I liked the old flat. The neighbours were fun and we'd painted all the walls black, and hung blankets over the windows. If you lay back on the bed you couldn't tell if your eyes were open or closed. It was like being dead. Chloe and I used to lie there for hours. It turned out that she liked the dark because she could pretend it was someone else with their fingers up my cunt, but I didn't know that so I was having a great time. I wished I hadn't thought about Chloe.

Phil said we should meet in town. When I first moved to Wales, coming back to Worcester felt great. But today I watched the brick houses rolling past, and the warehouses and car showrooms and canals and I just wasn't feeling it.

I knew I was a bit edgy about seeing Phil, but couldn't figure out why. I've known him and Jed forever. I used to go and see them in lunch hours, back when they were in the flat and I was at school. They were the only good thing then. And sometimes Chloe would be there when I arrived, in her girls grammar school gear, long skirt all rolled up at the waist. Pretending that she didn't care about kings and battles and algebra and whatever they do at posh schools. Pretending that what happened in the dark didn't count.

Phil and Jed do some labouring and that kind of stuff, but only when they need to and when someone will pay them. Jed has his own flat now, that he says he pays for himself. That's bollocks. He's from Cheltenham and his parents are rich and they're happy to bankroll him until he gets through this phase and grows up.

We only put up with Jed because he used to know a lot of people with money to spend on weed. It was great a few years back, but all his rich friends are buying coke now, and pills, and Phil and Jed are too old school to cope with all that. It's quite sweet. They bang on about cannabis being all pure and natural, but really it's because they're scared. Selling weed might not make them much money but they're white boys so it won't end them up in jail or getting stabbed either.

This way they can sit around, selling to kids and students and losers who think they're walking on the wild side. They can pretend that they're hard and cool. I thought they were too, when I was thirteen. Now I can see they're just big lazy idiots who can't be bothered to get a proper job. I love them though, and I'm pretty sure I'm making more money than them.

I got off the train at the end of the long platform. No shade anywhere. I pulled my sunglasses on. How you dress matters. You have to look like a cooler version of who you're selling to. Not intimidating, just cooler. In Llanyfenni, I had to be careful, they don't get out much, and I didn't want to alarm them. Totally different in Worcester. Different market.

Phil had said to meet at The Old Bank, by the bus station. That wasn't exactly my idea of a fun place to hang out, but I didn't say anything, which isn't like me. Maybe Angharad is a good influence. She doesn't say much and it's weirdly peaceful.

I'm not peaceful. I'm a worrier. Thoughts just buzz round my brain. They said at school to meditate instead of worrying. Maybe that helps with some stuff, but I don't see what. Just because you aren't worrying doesn't mean it won't happen, it just means that you won't be ready when it does.

That's another good thing about Llanyfenni, no school yet. My mum keeps saying she'll get it sorted but it's been a month *now and she's saying it less and less. Which saves her buying me all the uniform, and washing clothes, and means I can bring her a cuppa when she can't face getting out of bed, and clean the toilet when some bloke's pissed all over it, and roll her a joint if her hands are shaking too much. I don't mind, she's a mess. Someone needs to look after her.*

And I'm not the school type. All those girls stressing about whether their hair looks right, or who sent nudes to who.

Another bad thing about school was the early mornings. I'm no good in the mornings. I like to get out of the house sometimes in the evenings and walk. Sometimes I walk around all night and I don't know where I even am. In Worcester, I used to go along the canal. There's never anyone there late at night, just sometimes some sleepy ducks. You just have to watch for the dog shit. I hate dogs.

So back in Worcester, I was falling asleep in school and then all the teachers were all shouting at me. And mum and me have to be careful, because the last thing we need are people sniffing around and muttering about unstable home environments and crap like that.

Now, if it all gets a bit much at night, I head out of town and along the lanes. Sometimes I run. If I run fast enough and long enough sometimes I stop thinking and it's just me and the streetlights and the concrete and the tarmac, and then the fields and the sheep, on and on and on. And the sun's coming up and I know it means that I've got through another night. Now I can do what I want all night and sleep in the day when the house is quiet. No school is good for me.

When I got to the Old Bank, Phil was standing with a couple of blokes. They kind of looked me up and down the way blokes do. I knew I looked good, or as good as they were going to see. It's not hard, with blokes like that. They glanced at each other then one of the blokes nodded at Phil and then smiled at me. 'Get you a drink, babe?'

He wasn't a Worcester boy. Bristol, maybe. He had the

attitude too, like we were lucky that he was bothering with us.
'Brad,' he said, holding out his hand.

He had too many muscles. Not normal muscles, like Jake, from
shifting engines and hauling around bikes. More like too-many-
steroids muscles. And he was very tall. Like standing next to a
fridge. If a fridge was slightly twitchy. Good looking probably,
if you liked that sort of thing. I could tell I was going to hate
him.

He brought me a vodka over and we sat and talked shit for a
bit, like you do. The other guy, same white trainers, but no
muscles and dirty looking, was calling himself Jamie. He looked
like a liar to me. The kind of bloke that can't help but lie. I was
pretty sure I hated him too. I didn't worry about hiding it, until
I saw the way Phil was making big worried eyes at me. The
blokes didn't seem to care though. Maybe they were used to girls
looking at them like that so they just thought that was how girls'
faces always looked.

After I realised that Phil was stressing, I practised staring at
them as if they were fascinating. Pretended I thought they were
the centre of the fucking universe. Sometimes I see how over the
top I can go with looking adoring, waiting for a bloke, just one
fucking bloke, to realise I'm taking the piss. They never have.

They knew about the selling I was doing, they said they were
mates of Jed's. They said they'd heard about me, Jed had told
them, the hot young girl doing really well, making money all
over the place. Brad was chewing on his thumb, but stopped to
grin at me. 'Makes you laugh,' he said, 'There's people been at
university for years, making less dollars than we do.'

'Tossers in suits slogging their guts out,' Jamie agreed, 'With
their commuting and their little house in the suburbs and their
Ikea shit, making less than us,'

Phil nodded along, like he wasn't the sort of person who had
a little house in the suburbs. They all nodded at me approvingly.
'But you're doing great, babe. You're on your way. Nice one,
Phil.'

Phil looked chuffed. Like a cat that had brought its owner a dead bird. Or a mouse that was still squeaking and running about, but only for a matter of time. I downed my vodka. Swallowed the ice, even though it hurt.

After the blokes had left, we had a couple more drinks. It felt like we were celebrating. Like business men who'd signed some million dollar contract. I asked Phil who they were and he winked at me like that was an answer. I figured I'd get him to tell me later. Then we had a couple more. I remembered why I liked Phil and how much he made me laugh and I forgot to find out what was going on with those two slimeballs.

He asked about home and my mum again. So I told him about her, and how she was trying to keep it together, and Wales, and not being in school any more. 'So you're a free spirit?' he said, grinning, 'No one checking up on you?'

I raised my eyebrows, 'Free as the wind.' I grinned, 'Same again?'

'Nah, come on, let's get back up the road. Daria's been away. She's back and I don't want to wind her up.'

I didn't say anything about Daria. She was always wound up about something, which was fair enough. Either wound up and screaming or out of it and singing and dancing and talking about flowers and star signs. Phil fancied himself a bit of a Romeo around women. Not me, it wasn't like that with me, he knows me too well. Didn't normally stop blokes trying, but Phil got it. Probably after I kneed him in the balls after he walked in on me and Chloe, and then again after he tried to kiss me late one night, but fair play to him, he didn't need telling three times.

Mr Thomas

Some people, members of our congregation, aren't what we would hope. The sins of the flesh are evident, in some. Plastered across their faces, even on a Sunday. Lust in their eyes. But we gather them in, we gather in even the sinners, and together we will help them repent. I would spread my protection over them, as the Lord commands.

Faith

Broadway was just what I'd expected, tiny little boxes all the same. Weeds growing in the pavement. No trees. Why don't places like that have trees? When we got in, Phil showed me round, all proud of it. Every room painted some sort of cream, and someone had stuck up butterfly stickers. I didn't ask who. If it was Phil, I didn't want to know.

There was a proper bed, and the pillow cases matched the duvet cover and there were little pointless sequined cushions on the bed. I didn't say anything. I couldn't help rolling my eyes, but I didn't say anything.

The whole house was too hot, and the windows didn't open properly. We sat and had a can and Phil told me some bullshit story about having a gun under his pillow. I fell asleep on the settee. When I woke up, I could smell something good cooking and Daria was there. She was grumpy but she'd cooked a proper tea, roast beef and potatoes and it was magic. You never know with Daria, it could just have easily been cheese slices in pot noodle. Am not judging, pot noodles are good too, but it was nice to get some proper food. I told her that, and she calmed down a bit. Daria's sweet. She's nearly twenty but you wouldn't think it.

We had a bit of a chat later, when we were washing up. Their kitchen was too small for both of us really but I sat on the worktop and put things up in the top cupboards and we just chatted away about life and that. I'm good with girls too, not just men. 'I like your hair clip,'

Daria thinks she's really gifted. She likes sticking buttons and glitter on to stuff and giving it to people as presents. She'd given me a decorated jar for Christmas. Just for a second, when she handed me something wrapped in proper paper, I'd been thinking I might actually get a nice Christmas present. When I saw the jar, it was hard to know what to say. But I'd kept it. Phil gave me some weed later, but I wasn't sure if that was exactly a Christmas present. On the actual day, Mum had pissed the bed so I spent the morning cheering us up by telling her about celebrities' shitty boyfriends. It wa quite good fun in the end.

I suspected Daria had buttoned and glittered the hair clip herself too. She smiled shyly. 'I made it actually, Faith,'

I did my best to look surprised and impressed by her skill. She should stick to cooking, she isn't really much good at anything else. Definitely not drying up. She was wiping a mug with a sopping wet tea towel, which is pointless and disgusting. She was edgy tonight, which turned out to be because of Phil. No surprise. 'Has he said anything about me?' she looked at me, too intensely, 'Phil?'

Like I might possibly have thought she'd be worrying about anyone else. She stopped drying, putting all her energy into the staring. I was pretty sure Phil had said something about her, but I was way too fuzzy to remember what it might have been, and it probably wasn't anything she'd want to hear anyway. She carried on, without waiting for me to think of a lie, 'Do you think he loves me?'

I wasn't sure Phil was capable of love. And most straight ideas about love are a mystery to me anyway. It always seems to involve a lot of men behaving like arses and women crying. Maybe just the people I knew though, they probably weren't exactly representative. I shrugged.

'Because, Faith, I think I love him. Really love him.'

Her eyes filled with tears. I hurried up with putting plates away. She was still looking meaningfully at me, as if I could wave a magic wand and make Phil less of a douche. I was pretty sure I knew what was coming and I was right. 'But sometimes, I just think that maybe he isn't that committed, to me. To us.'

I thought about Phil, eyeing up barmaids in town, groping me, moaning about Daria cramping his style. Finding him fucking some hot red head in my bedroom, a few days before mum made us move. I thought about loyalty, to friends and to other girls. And about whether anything I would say would make any difference. And whether if she walked out, I would end up doing the cooking.

A tear rolled down her cheek, and I reached out to wipe it. She pulled back, eyes even wider, dropped the mug and the tea towel on the floor and ran out.

Once I'd finished in the kitchen, we all sat around and I got out the vodka I'd brought and we had a smoke and I still didn't remember to ask about the Bristol boys. Daria was busy painting henna on her arms. She was sitting very close to Phil and looking at me suspiciously every few minutes. Phil and I were watching Pingu on Youtube like I was twelve. In between watching Pingu, I was practising my Welsh in my head. Before we moved I didn't know that Welsh people really spoke Welsh, but they did in Llanyfenni and it was pretty embarrassing when the old boys were just chatting away between two different languages and I couldn't say anything. Gorsaf, I thought to myself. Dim parcio. Dim ysmygu. Pric. Jake was teaching me.

When I went to bed, I chucked the cushions on the floor and checked my phone to see if Angharad had been in touch. I knew she didn't have my number, but I was still kind of thinking she might find a way. I wondered if she was thinking about me, wondering where I was. Knew I was kidding myself. Tried not to think about the look of relief on her face when she realised I wasn't in church.

I had a million messages from Jake, sounding desperate. Bless. He was asking about weed, but I knew he wanted to see me just as much. He could get weed from anyone, but I make him feel like he's not a loser in a loser town. And I'm not too scary. Just show him a bit of fun. Though probably not as much as he'd like. I ignored his messages. I knew he'd be on my doorstep the minute I got back.

I lay back and shut my eyes. The pillows smelt of washing powder. I thought about money, trying to figure out how much Phil might owe me. So far, I had spent everything I'd earnt on stuff like the gas and electric. You pay more for gas and electric if you're on a meter, and even more if you need the emergency stuff. Money isn't mum's thing, so if I didn't help, we just ended up sitting in the dark. Once Mum got herself together, things would get better.

I woke up in the night. My heart was pounding fast and I felt jitters all through my body. I lay in the dark trying to figure out what had woken me up, but it was silent. There was no reason for me to feel so panicky. Everything was great.

Jamie

There's only two fucking rules, I told Brad. We don't smoke the product and we never inject. He just grinned like he was feeling sorry for me.

Angharad

Jake appeared back in my life the next day. My parents had left for work, so I was the only one home when the postman knocked. I hate answering the door. And I'm not allowed to, in case it's social services coming to see if I'm neglected. My dad might actually love that, because he could have a lovely chat with them about young people and explain all his theories about raising children autonomously, and show them some poetry about bats that I wrote when I was thirteen, but my Mum was firm about it. I am pretty obedient and less sure anyone would be impressed by the poem, so I didn't answer.

I did have a look out the window. The postman was filling in his little card about no-one being home, and Jake was sitting sideways on his bike pulled up at the kerb. He had his helmet under his arm and he was looking carefully at all the windows. When he saw me he started waving wildly. I shook my head at him and hid behind the door till the little card got posted through and then I gave it a couple more minutes and then opened the door. Jake was standing on the step. He looked down and up at my Snoopy nightie and fluffy slippers and raised his eyebrows. 'Come for a walk? I've been thinking.'

I dragged the nightie down. I really wanted to go for a walk, obviously. This was the sort of thing that was supposed to happen to teenagers.

I didn't want to turn my back on him and walk away in case he looked at me doing it. So I stood silently. 'Come on,' he said, bouncing on his toes, 'Get dressed. I'll wait here.'

And he turned and sat down on the step. I hoped neither of my parents drove past. As I walked up the stairs I could smell cigarette smoke. I tried to look at myself in the tiny bathroom mirror as I put on my sensible pants and my sensible bra. Wondered what underwear Ella wore. Or Faith. I suspected it didn't come from a mail order company in Devon, and wasn't chosen for being long lasting, environmentally friendly and modest. I put on my sensible skirt and my sensible t-shirt. Stopped looking in the mirror. There was no point. I was never going to look like those kind of girls. Maybe Jake would be won over by my sensible clothes and my morals.

We wandered towards the park. 'So what's the deal with you and Faith, then?' he asked, 'If you're not buying grass from her and you're not one of the dancing girlies?'

'Church,' I tried to sound friendly and welcoming and not defensive.

He kept right on walking, nodding a bit, as if he was thinking about it. 'Church,' he said eventually.

I wasn't sure if it was a question but I nodded anyway. Jake was still nodding away. 'Faith goes to church. Of course she does. Fucking brilliant. With her mum?'

I nodded. Jake was grinning away, like Faith and her mum at church was a joke. We passed a bench. 'Sit down while I roll up? Is that okay?'

I sat obediently, watching curiously. The hairs on his arms were very blond. His nails were disgusting. He looked like he was concentrating for a few minutes then lit up. 'You don't want one? Course you don't.. okay to keep walking?'

I jumped back up. I was behaving like a good dog. I hated myself. Jake was still thinking about Faith. 'So are you worried about her? Was she at church on Sunday? I guess church is a Sunday thing?'

'Yeah.. well, other stuff sometimes on other days.' I shut up. He probably didn't want a run down of the church timetable. I wasn't sure if I was betraying Faith, but I nodded anyway. 'Brilliant.' he said again.

He was blowing smoke up high, looking thoughtful. He was cooler than anyone I had ever known. 'So no one's seen her for at least a week.. just doesn't seem right. Not like her. I mean, if I was her friend I'd be worried.'

I felt judged. 'I'm not that much of a friend. Not a proper friend.' I said.

He was nodding again. Then he grinned. 'Looks like you and me might be the best she's got though. Come on, let's go and see what her mum thinks. If she's even noticed she's gone.'

'You said she was in a state on Thursday? Because she was worried about Faith?'

'Jeez, Angharad, I thought you'd met Marie? She might not even have noticed Faith's gone.' he smiled down at me, 'Don't worry, I'll look after you.'

I wondered why I'd need looking after.

Faith lived on a street around the back of town. I'd imagined drug dealers lived in some kind of scary flat. With a dog. Which would eventually get taken away by the police and put down when it bit off a toddler's face. Jake laughed again when I asked him if she actually definitely sold drugs, and ruffled my hair as if I was eight. 'Just marajuana. You're a sweetie,' he said, which I guess meant yes.

He knocked and walked in. The sitting room was straight inside the front door. I'd been scared about what it might be like inside too, but it was pretty much like my house except that there were plates and mugs lying round, and it smelt weird. Though I guess everyone got used to the way their house smelt. Maybe mine smelt weird too. Jake didn't seem to notice. 'Marie?' he called.

He seemed very comfortable here. I didn't like that but wasn't sure who I was jealous of, or why.

Faith's mum came and stood in the doorway. I was relieved that she looked the same as always. The way Jake talked about her had scared me a bit. She lifted her head at Jake, like a greeting, then smiled when she saw me. The smile was strange though, like she had to concentrate pretty hard on it. 'Hi, Angharad.'

'Hi,' I wasn't sure what to call her.

'Faith isn't home, I'm sorry,' she said 'Can I get you a drink? Tea?'

'Don't worry, Marie,' Jake smiled his charming smile, 'We won't bother you for long.'

'You're not a bother, Jake Morgan, you know that.'

Jake Morgan. I should have known. People talk about the Morgan brothers. Not bad things. Admiring things. I should have realised Jake was one of them. They're a bit like Llanyfenni's version of rock stars. Only because we don't have proper rock stars. No wonder Jake was so confident and so cool. Marie was leaning against the arm of the sofa. 'There's no point waiting for Faith, I'm not sure when she'll be back.'

She didn't look worried. I wondered if I should just leave, if she'd say more without me listening. Jake wasn't paying me any attention. 'Where is she, then?'

Marie looked a bit blank for a second. 'You know what teenage girls are like. Maybe she's gone to the pool. She keeps herself very fit.'

Jake looked a bit taken aback at the idea of Faith swimming. I was too, really. I couldn't remember the last time I went to our swimming pool, not since I was about six. Maybe that was where Llanyfenni's druggies hung out. At the pool and having dance lessons. I wondered if I actually knew anything about Llanyfenni or anyone who lived there.

Jake moved on. 'Marie, is she in town? Or has she gone to Worcester?'

Marie shrugged. 'Worcester, I think. I thought she was going to see Phil. She's not answering her phone though.' Marie stopped for a second and then looked like she was changing gears inside her head. 'She'll be back when she's hungry. She wouldn't leave me. She always comes back.'

I didn't know if Jake found that any more convincing than I did. Faith wasn't a cat.

Jake managed to stay focussed. 'How long's she been gone?'

'She said she was going on Sunday, she was in a right mood when she came home from the steam thing in the park' – I pretended not to see the significant look Jake gave me – 'but you know what the trains are like here, she had to wait till Monday. Or maybe Tuesday. I don't know, Jake, all the days are the same here.'

She looked worried, and Jake nodded reassuringly. 'I know what you mean.'

I felt cross. I was sure Jake knew nothing about the trains here. He probably just drove everywhere on his motorbike, spreading dangerous fumes, giving people asthma and buying cannabis. He sat down next to her on the settee, and gave me a stern look. I wasn't sure where I was supposed to sit. Everything looked dirty. I ignored his look and he smiled at Marie. 'Has she called you at all, Marie?'

'I gave her a call on Thursday, or maybe Friday, when I couldn't find my prescriptions, but she didn't answer so I guess she's busy,'

I wasn't sure if Marie sounded a bit defensive, I couldn't believe a normal mum would let her daughter go to Worcester whenever she felt like it, let alone lose her daughter and not feel embarrassed if someone pointed it out. I expected Jake to give her a lecture like he'd given me but he just said, 'I'm up that way in a couple of days, I was going to call by, say hi.'

Marie nodded, 'Well, if she's not there, Phil would help you out. I'll give you his number.'

Jake put the number in his phone, and thanked her. 'Marie, are you keeping okay?' he asked her quietly. I stood by the door, waiting to leave. I didn't hear what she told him, but he gave her a quick hug and we finally headed off.

We set off down the road. I was hungry. And my head

ached. Jake was silent. I didn't want to sound like a whingy kid so I kept quiet too. If I didn't mess it up again, he might forget about the snotty crying in Cafe Sosban and the Snoopy nightie.

He strode back towards the park. I hurried along, trying to look like I was an equal partner in this relationship. I'd given up on Jake thinking I was the kind of girl he usually hung out with, but I was still hoping someone would see us and jump to the wrong conclusions. Also, I thought smugly, no one would mistake me for the kind of girl that he only liked because they were slutty. We sat back down on the bench. 'So what happened last Sunday, then?' Jake looked at me.

'What do you mean?'

'Sunday, Angharad. Her mum said she was stressed and she went to the fair. Sunday is the day she gets dressed up and goes to church, you said. So you saw her in the morning.'

'She doesn't dress up. Not properly.'

'I bet she doesn't.' Jake pursed his beautiful lips, and lost focus for a second. 'So Sunday is the day Faith goes to church looking hot, you all look down your noses at her for not wearing a smock, and then you all pray to be better people. And then what happened?'

'She asked me to go to the rally.' I tried to sound casual, like it wasn't the most exciting thing that had happened to me since I found the Sylvanian Family narrowboat in the Red Cross shop.

'No way!' Jake looked enchanted, 'I was there with Morgan Bikes! Did you see?'

'No,' I lied, trying not to think of my heart, tarnishing with all the sinning I was doing.

'And Faith was going to be dancing there, she said. With Ella.'

Jake's eyes went a bit unfocussed again. 'Have you seen Faith dance?'

I shook my head. 'Anyway,' Jake seemed to pull himself together from whatever he was picturing in his head, 'What happened at the rally?'

'She kissed me. We kissed each other,'

Jake tipped his head on the side and peered at me, raising his eyebrows. He was so gorgeous I could hardly breathe. I didn't fancy him. It was just a fact. 'Of course you did,' he was nodding again. 'Must have been some kiss if she wanted to leave the country straight after.'

He thought for a minute again. 'You want to tell me about it?'

He nodded encouragingly, head tipped over like a dog wanting a biscuit.

'Well..' I wasn't sure where to start, 'we sat down and then we were sort of looking at each other –'

'Whoa!' He seemed appalled, 'I was joking. Angharad, you need to learn some rules. That stuff's private. You can't go round snogging girls and telling everyone all the details. It's just not respectful.'

He seemed to be laughing at me again but I wasn't sure. I wished I hadn't told him anything. I wished I hadn't gone to the rally. Everything had got very complicated. I wasn't sure if I was wishing Faith had never turned up at church. In her short dress. Or if I wished that I hadn't noticed her short dress. And her long brown legs.

Jake seemed to have been thinking a bit too. 'So you thought she was my girlfriend and you made a move on her? Because that's pretty low, Angharad. Do I need to watch out for you?'

He was still watching me. It was disconcerting. He had such beautiful eyes. When he looked at me, it was like he could see me naked. Not just my body, my mind too. I could feel myself going red again. 'No! I wasn't thinking anything about you!'

Which was nearly true. 'I didn't know you. But then Ella

said Faith had gone away with you.'

'You know Ella's full of shit?'

'Isn't she your girlfriend then?'

He still hadn't looked away, and even though I wanted to, I didn't either. He had very long eyelashes. His pupils were huge, staring into mine. He shrugged a bit. 'Well, it's complicated.'

And then he did look away. And I was pretty sure that meant that Faith was right, about what she'd said at the park on Sunday. And I felt a bit sorry for Ella. I could see why anyone might hope that Jake would be your boyfriend. But even I could see that it would take more than blowjobs.

After we talked, Jake had to head off, he was meeting someone. He didn't say who. I'd given him my number. He seemed to assume I would. I walked home slowly.

The house was empty. I poured some cereal, took it out to the garden with a blanket and fell asleep.

When I woke up the sun was in a completely different place. My face felt hot and horrible, my mouth was dry. I still had a headache and I still hadn't figured out how I felt about anything – about Jake, the drugs, Faith disappearing and definitely not about kissing her. I felt all wrong, like I didn't even know who I was any more.

I had a text from Jake. 'Sorry if I freaked you out today x'

I went to get a drink and get out of the sun, and look at myself in the mirror to see if I was massively sunburnt. My face was totally bright red. I covered it in cold water and moisturiser and drank a load more cold water and managed to wait another five minutes before I answered Jake. I didn't want to be like other girls, hassling him. 'No problem,' I sent. And then, to show that I cared about Faith, 'Did you speak to Phil?'

I spent the next hour hanging about near my phone while Jake didn't reply.

Part of me wished I'd taken Phil's number too, but I was

pretty sure I wouldn't have been brave enough to actually phone him. I wondered if I could find him on Facebook. I hadn't found Faith. Maybe drug dealers didn't use Facebook. I tried searching. There were loads of Jake Morgans. None looked like him. We had no mutual friends. No big surprise. I found Morgan Display Team and spent forty minutes staring at photos of Jake jumping through flames and over members of the public. Or it could have been his brother. I couldn't really tell them apart with their helmets on.

My mum came home and asked about my day. I didn't mention Jake or going to Faith's house or Faith's mum being a bit weird. I did tell her I'd fallen asleep in the garden and not done any maths or English or science. She sighed at me.

Considering I wasn't allowed in school because of the fossils and evolution, it seemed a bit rich to suddenly expect me to have such a passion for science I'd study it alone every day (but still ignoring the fossils and evolution and anything ungodly). After years of enthusiastic parenting, my mum and dad seemed to have gone off the boil a bit when I reached puberty. Sink or swim, seemed to be the new philosophy. Sink or swim, but keep praying a lot. No questioning God but also pass a physics GCSE. Compared to all that, getting my head around accidentally kissing a drug dealer and going for coffee with a stunt biker probably should have been easier.

I had thought that I might talk to my dad. After tea, we usually play chess together and he tells me about his day. Sometimes it feels like we're both pretending, my dad showing me what a good dad he is, and me saying vague things about plant cells and Shakespeare to imply that I've been busy all day learning the sorts of things he thinks I'm good at. My dad might say all sorts of things about not judging people, but you can't forgive people for their faults without making a few decisions about what counts as faults.

It was after midnight when Jake replied. I'd left my phone by my bed so it would wake me. *'Phil says everythings cool x'*

I sat up crossly. What did that mean? And why didn't he use an apostrophe? Maybe he didn't know how. I replied 'Is Faith with him then?'

Then I sat in the darkness waiting for him to reply. I fell asleep before he did. I dreamt that I could hardly breathe because my mouth was full of strawberries.

Mr Thomas

Any parent knows, and any child knows, that a father has a different heart than a mother does. They are both God's love, but they are different. Every child has the right to a two-parent family. Without the love of a father, a child can not grow truly. I pray for the children from families which are broken. It's not like Marie even chose to come to Llanyfenni. She just washed up here, as far as I can tell. Washed up and now our community must take her in as one of our own.

Faith

So it was a few days after that my phone went missing. No biggie, in a way. It had been a weird sort of week. Fun, at first. I hung out some days with Jed at his swanky new flat by the old docks. The flat was pretty cool. Apart from his furniture. And he had Jamaican flags hanging in his bedroom, and bongos in the corner and a Bob Marley poster. Moody black and white photo of some French film star. A selection of bongs. You have to feel sorry for Jed, it's like he had this idea when he was ten about what he'd do when he was grown up and just never reassessed. He did have Netflix though. And Amazon Prime. And a massive TV.

It did make me feel sad for my mum, that I was choosing Netflix and Amazon and vodka over her. Thought for two seconds that maybe I should go back. Stared out the balcony doors, down at the boats. Thought about my mum, bobbing about like someone had cut her ropes. Maybe moving was a mistake. At least in Worcester she'd had friends. I should have talked her out of it, instead of taking her to the library and showing her how the websites worked and all the houses we could exchange with. And I definitely could have done a bit of research, instead of telling her to take the first thing that was offered. Maybe in our old flat some girl from Llanyfenni is thinking the same.

Then Jed shouted through from the kitchen that he was making bacon sarnies, and did I want one and Orange is the New Black had a new series out, and that was pretty much that. No contest. Netflix, weed and bacon sarnies and I would have a couple of days off from thinking about my mum. Respite, the social workers used to call it. A bit of relaxation, and then I'd totally go back and sort her out.

I had been ready to be pissed off with Jed. Years ago, we had sorted out who was in charge between us, and it was me. I was smarter than him, and prettier and no one thought I was a wanker. But for the last few months, it was like he was trying to change things about. He'd been sending some strange texts. Telling me to sell more, links to sales seminars on YouTube and sometimes photos of himself smiling and doing a thumbs up when I told him what I'd sold. I ignored him, mainly, but it was annoying. As soon as he saw me, he was on my case. 'Have you met Brad and Jamie?'

I shrugged. 'White guys in white t-shirts? One looks a bit like a gerbil? Like this?'

I screwed up my face and started tapping my foot to look like some Bristol guy on too many steroids. Jed didn't laugh. 'Yeah, I met them,' I said, in case he didn't recognise my impression.

'What did you think?'

'Are they why you're being weird?'

'Not being weird, Faith. Do you think I'm being weird?'

I shook my head. It's always better to be nice to Jed when he says stuff like that, otherwise he just gets worse. But I did think he was being weird. 'I'm just trying to do better. Have some goals. That's not weird.'

That didn't sound like Jed. I'd always assumed he had goals even it was mainly trying to convince people that he was practically Jamaican and brought up on a council estate, but this sounded more like aspirational Instagram goals. 'Are you sure?'

He looked pissed off. I shrugged. 'Okay. Goals. Nice one. Selling any molly yet?'

He lifted a dumbbell and started waving it about, as if that was going to impress anyone. 'You can make money from weed. You don't need to get into all that unnatural crap.'

I wondered who he was trying to convince. I mean, I felt like I made money, but I was fifteen. It paid for some of the bills and the trainers, but it wasn't exactly a long-term career strategy. If you wanted to make serious, grown up money, so your parents weren't paying your rent and you didn't have to go out shifting bricks when business was slow, then you needed to be selling coke. Or smack. Everyone knew that. I was technically a child and I knew that.

I turned the TV on and ate my sandwich. I didn't thank him, just in case we were still having some hierarchy issues. 'Is there anything you want to tell me?'

I knew I sounded like a teacher. I bent over so he could see my tits, to take the edge off it. He shook his head.

Selling has got loads easier since Snapchat. Except that people don't really want hash anymore, and they can be a bit snotty about haze. We had the doors open onto the balcony, and the wind kept blowing the cash about. It was ace. I took a photo, but Jed wouldn't let me post it in case people thought about nicking it. Jed asked how Marie was, what she was up to, if she had a boyfriend, if I was making friends, going to school. Told me about how cool it was that I had seen a bit more of the country now, and how cool it would be if I got to travel around more. I ignored that, patronising shit.

I saw a load of people I hadn't seen for ages. They all hung around and we watched Paw Patrol and Peppa Pig and it was just like the old days. Every so often, I'd cook up a load more bacon and anyone who was around would be eating sandwiches and laughing at Daddy Pig. Now, when I smell bacon, it always makes me think of Worcester. Everyone smiling and laughing. Because we were stoned, and I didn't know what was coming next, but it was still a nice memory.

I'm very good at selling weed. In Llanyfenni, I'm always having to make sure mum's not too weird, not freaking anyone out. It was a lot easier in Worcester, with Jed. Even though he's posh and annoying, he's not going to start coming on to some fourteen year old boy, or start trying to put up the Christmas tree. Or announce that he's pregnant and start crying. I remember that I don't need to think about Mum. Feel pissed off that she's sneaked into my brain again. And when I told Jed that it was nicer selling here than at Marie's, he looked relieved. Which was weird. 'Really?' he asked, as if he had never met

Marie. 'You're growing up, I guess, ready to start out on your own.'

That wasn't exactly what I'd meant.

At Jed's, you could cook as much as you wanted because he's not on a meter and you could just lie on the carpet if you wanted because you could tell by the smell that no one had pissed on it. No one had pissed on the bathroom floor either, or on the toilet seat. I was living the piss-free dream in Worcester. I hadn't ever had a holiday, but this was pretty close. Sun shining and the sweet smell of hash. Lying on the balcony with the warm breeze in the evening, and the sun setting behind the old warehouses. Listening to Jed ramble on about all his crazy conspiracy theories was worth it.

Other days, I hung out with Phil in Broadend. Phil used to be lush. I used to be able to tell him anything. But for some reason I didn't want to mention Angharad. Or that Mum had dragged me along to a church. He asked if I'd heard from Chloe. I laughed in his face. 'Did you think I'd still be hung up on her? She wasn't that great, Phil.'

It was true, too. Phil ruffled my hair. 'And has your mum called?'

I shrugged. I didn't want to remember watching the phone vibrating and ignoring it. 'Tell me what's going on with Jed?'

Turned out, like I'd thought, that the guys that were stressing out Jed were the same guys I'd seen in The Old Bank, Brad and Jamie. No one knew where they came from. Like the mafia or something, they just rocked up in town one day. There's a load of rumours, but everyone was making money out of them so no one was asking too many questions. They brought weed up from Bristol, sold it cheap. 'Other stuff too,' Phil said, 'pills and coke and that.'

Anyway, Jed and Phil were selling for Brad and Jamie now, so I guess I was too. Phil was a bit pissy because he'd had a text from Jake. He was kind of lecturing me. 'You need to look after your customers,' he said, like he's on The Apprentice or something.

I couldn't be bothered to explain how ignoring Jake was definitely the right thing to do. 'It's just Jake.'

He looked all disapproving. 'You need to answer texts, and deliver straight away.'

I stuck my finger up at him. I thought he'd laugh, but he carried on looking stern. 'That's what Brad says.'

'Well, I can't deliver anything if I'm here,' I told him.

Phil nodded. 'Brad's right,' he said. 'You're a smart cookie.'

'Fuck Brad,' I said, but I said it to myself.

After that, I decided I definitely wouldn't answer any texts. Didn't even look at Insta, or Snapchat. I knew what I was doing.

So apart from Phil's massive crush on Brad, it had all been good, with Jed and Phil. And Daria. We were like a happy little family, and dinner on the table at five. Loads of food, pies and steak and proper school dinner stuff. Daria and I took turns cooking, and when she was too spaced out and I couldn't be bothered, we had noodles or takeaway. Indian, or Chinese or pizza, whatever we wanted. In Llanyfenni, there's only one Indian restaurant and it's always empty because the hygiene rating on the door is one.

Jamie

It took Brad less than 2 weeks to pick up a £50 a day crack habit. That's when we had to get serious. I love him, he's good people, but fuck. There was no going back then.

53

Brad

I like to tell customers the truth. Tell them about the massive hard-ons and wanking till you bleed. We're all brothers. Down this hole together. I think they like that.

Jamie

This is a bloody nightmare.

Angharad

When I woke up, my first thought was to worry that I'd missed Jake's text. I hadn't. He just hadn't replied. Even though he must still have been awake, surely. Now I knew why Reddit had so many threads about trying to understand men.

Then I started worrying about Faith. It all seemed even stranger in the morning. I didn't know why Marie didn't seem bothered. It wasn't right. Someone should be thinking about Faith and Jake had implied it was him and me. We'd been a team. Now I seemed to be on my own. I didn't understand what I'd done wrong or why he hadn't answered. I felt confused but not surprised. Just another part of life that there turned out to be rules for. Rules that I didn't know.

I was watching New Girl when my phone tinged. I knew it was either Jake or my mum because no-one else even had my number. I felt my tummy do a little excited flip when Jake's name came up. 'Calm down,' I told it firmly.

'Park in 15 x'

Jake's abbreviated texts were flustering. But at least he was alive. And he wanted to see me. I figured I better reply so he knew I'd seen it, and then wandered along to the park. Jake was waiting for me, sitting on a picnic bench. He leapt off when he saw me, and came loping across the grass. 'Hey,' he said, with his disconcertingly charming grin. 'What's up? And what's happened to your face? It's bright red.'

I felt like I was blushing again, but at least he probably couldn't tell through the sunburn. 'Jake, shouldn't you be at work?'

'No, Mum,' he grinned some more. 'Tea break. Elevensies. Whatever. I wanted to see you. You sounded pissed off.'

My useless heart skipped at how well he knew me already. 'What did Phil say?'

'He said it was cool. I told you. So you can stop worrying,'
'Was that all?'
'He offered to sort something out if I was up that way. You know, that kind of stuff. Stuff you disapprove of, Mrs Stroppy Pants,' he winked cheerily. 'So it's all cool. But don't keep texting me, okay? Ella gets pissy.'
'But you were texting me!'
'Yeah, yeah,' he was nodding again, grinning away, 'but, y'know, just don't text back. I mean, she hears it buzzing, and just grabs it and then freaks out.'
'Right.' I tried to look like I understood what was happening. Thought about what he'd said. 'So you didn't actually speak to Faith?'
'I text Phil, like we said. And Phil text back. Maybe it was Faith texting. It's the kind of thing she'd say.' He thought for a minute. 'Yeah, it could have been Faith.'
'But what if it was Phil and he was lying?'
'Jesus, Angharad! Why would he lie?'
I shrugged, feeling embarrassed. But I knew it wasn't impossible. People do lie. Jake was still looking at me as if I was the strangest person he had ever met in his life. 'I guess Faith's probably just had enough of this crummy town and gone back to where the action is.'
'Why would she do that?'
He shrugged. 'I'm not a psychiatrist, Angharad,' he said. 'Maybe because she made a mistake and snogged a girl she fancied who turned out to be a bit of an uptight snob. Maybe she was worried you'd be blabbing about it all over town. No offence, Angh, but that's probably what happened. I mean, you told me all about it the first time you met me, she probably knows what you're like.' He paused, nodding a bit.
I felt dizzy, like he'd punched me. 'You think she didn't trust me?'
'Well, put it like this, I wouldn't tell you anything I

wanted keeping private. And you're a bit of a troublemaker, let's be honest. You've already stressed out Ella.'

I still didn't say anything. He reached over and ruffled my hair gently. 'Right, I'll get going. Do you fancy a drink later?'

'A drink?'

'Don't worry, I'll buy them.' He shook his head, laughing at me. 'I can't see you getting served!'

I was too confused to properly appreciate being asked out for a drink by one of the Morgan brothers. 'But Jake, aren't you worried about Faith?'

He screwed his forehead up. 'Nah. I don't think so. Not anymore. But if you want, we can get the train up, check it out?'

'The train?'

'Yeah, you know, woo woo.' He did a bad impression of a train's whistle.

'You and me?'

'Yeah, if you want? I'm not doing anything Monday. Going out for the day'd be better than a drink anyway. I won't take you on the bike, it's not your kind of thing. Can we do it in a day on the train? There and back?'

'I don't know!' I wasn't sure if I was infuriated. 'Won't Ella be angry?'

He sighed, as if I was being naive. 'She can't read my texts if I'm not with her, can she, Angh? Check out the train times? Okay, catch you later. Sort it out and let me know what time. Come here, babes.'

And he put his arms around me, and gave me an enthusiastic, oily, aftershavy hug, then loped off again towards the town. I sat down on the bench. Wondered if the bike was Ella's kind of thing. If she sat behind him and wrapped her arms around him. And I was more the type of person you got the train with. Like old people and kids. And could you go to Worcester and back in a day on our train? I googled. Worcester turned out to only be three hours away, and there were four a day each way. I fantasized briefly about breakfast on the train with Jake, or sitting holding coffees in the dawn sunlight. I text him straight away with the details, and told him we should get the six o'clock train so we had as much time as possible. Surely Ella wasn't reading his texts at work. He replied with a kiss.

I passed one of the home educated GCSE girls – Sara – on the way home. 'Hey,' I said, hoping that she had seen me with Jake, forgetting she was a bitch.

She looked surprised, briefly, then smiled back. 'Hey, Angharad.'

Maybe not a complete bitch, I decided.

I sat in the kitchen waiting for my mum to come home. She looked tired. I told her I was going to Worcester for the day. She looked quite worried, as if I was a toddler. 'On your own?'

I should have thought of how I would explain suddenly needing to go to Worcester. I tried to think of a reason anyone would suddenly need to go to Worcester. Though Google said there was a nice cathedral. I didn't want to lie. We aren't a lying sort of family. 'Faith is staying there, we thought we might meet up.'

And I couldn't help but see a flash of relief in her eyes. However much she knows that she is right about me being better than the other kids she knows, she can't disguise how much she would like me to have a friend. It took me a minute to realise the feeling that I was having was hurt. I kept talking. 'I'll have my phone, there's only one change, and I'll get the train home just after six.'

She scrunched up her forehead again, but like she was pretending to be worried now. I said, 'We'll just go shopping and hang out and stuff. I'll be in the middle of Worcester.'

Now it felt like we were both pretending that I was a rebellious teenager. I wished that I didn't know that she was already anticipating casually mentioning at work that her daughter had gone shopping with a friend. In a city. Understood that I had been half-hoping that she would stop me. She was washing her hands, opening the fridge. Pretending not to have already decided that however worried she was about Worcester and Faith, that it was easily outweighed by the idea that I might be normal. 'There's all sorts of people in Worcester.'

'I know. I'll be fine. I'll take my rape alarm.'

I could tell that she was already lost in a little daydream. Now I had a friend, I might get another. And then be in a pipeline of fitting in and doing GCSEs and heading off to university. And then she would know that she had been right all along and the other home ed mums would be humble but also friendly, in the face of her evident superiority. In her day dream, Faith had probably morphed into a much more respectable girl, who could play the clarinet and enjoyed fun Christian youth social events. Almost the polar opposite to the Faith in my day dreams, who was either chained up and scared in a dungeon or naked. Or both. I hated myself for that.

I walked upstairs feeling like I might be sick. I would go to Worcester, with sexy Jake, find Faith and check she was all fine. Apparently I was the only one who knew that I was completely out of my depth.

Faith

Daria and I were in the kitchen drinking tea when Jed turned up. The door was on the latch so he just walked in. I didn't even notice he was there till I realised Daria was standing there with her mouth wide open. Jed was a mess. He can be sweaty anyway and it was hot outside, but he was dripping all over the lino. His face was even whiter than usual. He didn't say anything. I felt my heart go funny, realised that my mouth was open too.

Then Phil walked in, and we started moving. Daria went to rub his back and I walked over to the fridge and grabbed him a can.

When he took it, his hands were shaking. Even Phil seemed quiet. 'Mate!'

Jed nodded. 'They're mental, Phil.'

Daria made big eyes at Jed and then at me. 'It's okay,' I said.

It wasn't exactly news to me that my mum had her issues, or that Jed had a pretty limited vocabulary. 'Who?' I asked, which seemed like the more important thing.

Jed was looking at me, then at Phil. 'What?' I asked.

'You want to come outside?' Phil said, and I noticed he was talking to Jed. Definitely not to me. Or to Daria.

Jed didn't say anything, but he moved towards the back door. As soon as they shut it behind them, Daria and I moved to the window. Jed seemed to take a while to get going, and to be staring at the ground a lot. Daria put the kettle on. 'Poor Jed,' she said.

I wasn't so sure. 'Who do you think freaked him out?'

She shrugged. 'You know what Jed's like. He's a worrier.'

'He's paranoid.'

'None of us are perfect, Faith.'

I tipped my head forwards against the window. They were still shuffling about out there, looking away from the house. I could hear next door's kids squealing, but nothing that Jed was saying. I breathed steam onto the window. 'I bet it's Jamie and Brad.'

When she didn't answer, I moved so that I could see her. She was getting mugs out of the cupboard, slowly. 'Daria?'

She shrugged. Her dreads were tied up with a her big red clip, she looked like a little doll. 'I think we need to let Phil and Jed handle this. You know what men are like.'

I turned back to the window before I rolled my eyes.

Later, when Phil had lit the barbie and Jed was drunk, I followed him when he went inside. I didn't know if he noticed me. He went into the toilet and I stood outside. I wanted to know what was going on. He was still edgy and he wasn't saying much. I didn't understand why he didn't just go home, if he didn't want to be here. Phil kept pouring me vodka, which should have been a good thing but something about it felt desperate. I drank it anyway, seemed rude not to.

When he finally came out, it took a minute before he twigged that it was me. 'Faith.'

He had one eye screwed up, like he was trying not to see me. 'What's going on, mate?' I asked.

'Just Brad and Jamie.' He shrugged. 'You know what they're like.'

I didn't, really. Had only met them once. I wasn't convinced that they were actually that impressive. I thought I could probably scare Jed, if I tried, and I'm not six foot of twitchy muscle. And it seemed a bit weird for any kind of gangster to be that fussed about Jed. There had to be more useful people to be bothering round here. I thought that Jed was the kind of person you might threaten if you were too weak to take on the actual big boys. But there was no point spoiling things for Phil and Jed, they were so sure they were taking a step up and joining the scary gangsters. Seemed kinder to just let them live in their fairytale.

It wasn't very nice, but if Jamie and Brad had been trying to get Jed to pull himself together, I was on their side. I could see that sweaty, drunk Jed banging on at customers in a pretend accent that he thought sounded Jamaican and asking a load of questions – 'What's the government for?', 'Is the sunset just, like, pure energy?' – and playing his bongos probably wasn't much help if you were trying to make serious money. Even I got pissed off with him, and I actually liked him.

He skirted past me and went back outside. I leant back on the worktop. The smell of the barbie made me think of burgers and the taste of Angharad. Made me think of the way that she looked at me in the park. The way she looked before we kissed, not after, when she just looked like she might have a panic attack. Maybe I shouldn't have left her, it'd be awkward if she had. I tried not to imagine her nice, squidgy cheeks all sweaty and pale.

And suddenly I was so worried about her it hurt. I couldn't believe how much I wanted to see her, to explain why I'd run off, maybe say sorry if I'd messed things up with her. I was looking at my phone, wondering if I could call her. Hear her funny Welsh voice. Check she was okay.

I went to have a piss. Daria followed me in. 'Faith?'

'Yup?'

She leant against the wall, maybe trying to look cute. She did look cute. If you liked someone who seemed to base her entire personality on an anime character. 'I didn't mean to be rude... before. I've just never –'

'Never?'

I was trying to hurry things along. I figured I knew where this was going. She opened and shut her mouth a bit, like a sexy goldfish. 'Never thought about – you know – girls.'

I looked at her. She's short, but so am I, so we were pretty much staring straight into each other's eyes. I leant back against the wall, let her do the work. She opened her mouth again, and then stepped forward. Her lips were soft and slippy with scented lip balm. I wondered if she'd chosen cherry cola specially. I let her put her hands on my hips, pull herself close to me. Wondered why I let girls behave like this, as if I owed them it. Afterwards, she looked at me shyly, as if we shared a secret. 'Phil is going to freak,' she said happily, and skipped off back outside.

I rolled my eyes at myself in the bathroom mirror.

When I got back outside, my phone had disappeared. Phil and Jed were still very busy with the barbeque and Daria was standing near Phil, looking through her eyelashes at me. I looked around on the grass, and asked if anyone had seen it, but apparently nobody had.

I couldn't help feeling Brad and Jamie should have words with Phil as well as Jed, the pair of them were a fucking liability.

Angharad

On Saturday night it had finally started raining. Only drizzle, but it was still drizzling on Sunday morning. Sam didn't go out in church so I didn't either. I hoped it was because of the drizzle and not because he hated me now. I don't think he looked at me, but I didn't want to make it weird by looking at him too much to check.

It was a long service. I had forgotten what church was like when you actually sat through it. I liked the singing though. And I wanted to see what was going on with Marie. I saw quite a few of the church people seemed to be politely saying a few words and then moving away. They were very careful to stay smiling and friendly. I might not have noticed if I wasn't used to reading the special church body language and I wasn't watching so closely.

Marie was sitting next to Cerys, who possibly hadn't noticed the special polite treatment Marie was being given. Marie still looked subdued. She kept her eyes low and stayed close to Cerys. When the service ended they left together, almost straight away. And then I saw my mum looking after them, with her concerned expression.

I realised my dad was watching too. 'What do you think?' he asked my mum.

They had obviously been talking about Marie, privately. I wondered if I should tell them about Marie being a bad mum, not caring about Faith. Mr Thomas came bustling over. My dad shook his hand. That's the kind of thing people do in our church. My mum smiled, politely. I smiled too, to show that I was pleased to talk to him. Even if I wasn't really. Being in church seemed to involve a lot more polite dishonesty than when I wasn't in church. But at least with church, I understood the rules.

'Angharad,' Mr Thomas said solemnly, maybe to show he remembered my name.

It sounded like a warning. Like I was on a list of possible sinners and he was keeping an eye on me. I suspected Mr Thomas was going to be annoying. But it was true that I was sinning quite a lot, especially in my head, when I thought about Faith and Jake. I felt a bit rebellious. It was hard to see that thinking a bit about Faith naked equated to proper sins, like stealing. I knew this was not the sort of thinking my mum approved of. But I stayed where I was, polite and smiling, because I did want to know what he and my parents thought was going on with Marie.

Usually not much happens in church, apart from one of the old people dying. Or someone buying the wrong biscuits for the tea and biscuits afterwards. (Anything fancy and chocolate, if you're wondering. Anything fancy at all is basically disapproved of in our church. It's why the old people have got such bad knees, probably, years of kneeling righteously on the cold stone floor. They can't walk very well, but they know they've suffered enough to be welcome in heaven. Probably in some special VIP area for the specially righteous who've suffered especially hard. From choice, not like, say, homeless people. And they say tea and biscuits, but it's tea and just one biscuit really, unless you want to be the person everyone's whispering about the next Sunday).

Mr Thomas was looking around, all bulging eyes like a sheep that's about to get sheared. I guessed that meant that he didn't want anyone to hear. I gazed off into the distance. When I was younger, that was the best way to hear what the adults were saying without them noticing. I wasn't sure it would still work, but then I heard Mr Thomas mutter fiercely. 'I'm terribly worried. Marie seems to be a bit of a troubled soul.'

Out of the corner of my eye, I watched my dad nod thoughtfully. He didn't say anything. I could tell my mum was itching to share some opinions, but for some reason in church it's mainly the men that talk. I was starting to wonder if that was such a good idea, seeing as so many men seemed totally oblivious to most of what went on in Llanyfenni. Mr Thomas looked around and then carried on muttering, 'We have prayed a lot. All of us.'

I couldn't help feeling that was a bit unfair. The whole church talking about Marie, and her knowing nothing about it. 'Cerys and Marie are spending a lot of time together,' my dad agreed. 'We are all very fond of Cerys, especially Angharad, but she can be a bit confused.'

I pretended to be studying a stained glass window with Jesus next to a lamb. I didn't want to announce that I was not fond of Cerys and I had no idea why they were all so convinced that I was. It did annoy me though.

Mr Thomas started up again, getting to the point. Or what I suspected was the point for the church. 'We are worried that Marie may be led astray by bad thoughts. You may not know but Cerys is rather wealthy.'

Cerys being wealthy seemed a bit unlikely but I figured Mr Thomas probably knew what he was talking about. My church always seems pretty hot on the state of its members' finances. And if Cerys was rich and Marie knew, then I guessed she might be being led astray by bad thoughts. I couldn't believe someone who let their daughter behave like Faith did would think twice about taking poor, old Cerys's money if she could. And everyone knew that old people were very bad about knowing who to trust.

My dad said carefully, 'It would just be nice to know a bit more about Marie, so we can put any doubts the congregation is feeling to rest. Angharad?'

I suspected my dad hadn't been fooled by my interest in stained glass, especially when I'd seen it every week of my life. I looked at him, polite and smiling. He explained to Mr Thomas. 'Angharad is friends with Marie's daughter.'

Mr Thomas turned red at the mention of Faith. I suspected he disapproved even more of Faith and her short skirts than of her mum. I hoped it was disapproval, anyway. I hoped he didn't have the same sinful thoughts about Faith's short skirts that I did. I found myself shuffling back a bit. When I thought about it, I didn't think I liked Mr Thomas much. He humphed a bit. My dad intervened. 'Do you know much about Marie, cariad?'

I wanted them to understand, to see that Faith hadn't been looked after like a normal person. 'I don't think she's a very good mum.'

They all nodded approvingly and I felt suddenly guilty. 'Maybe you could go round and visit her?' Mr Thomas said, as if he was suggesting it from charity, as if I hadn't just listened to him fretting about Marie stealing Cerys's money.

I shook my head. I didn't want to know any more about Marie. I was sure the church would look after Cerys, hopefully with something more than prayer. I was pretty sure they would, especially if they thought that without Marie's involvement her money might eventually end up in the new roof fund. And my dad isn't the sort of person to let little old ladies have their money taken, in any circumstances. 'Well, Angharad,' Mr Thomas did his special meaningful sheep look again, 'if you happen to hear anything useful, then please do feel able to come and talk to me.'

If, for example, Marie decided to share her plan to steal thousands from an old lady with me, seemed to be what he was implying. Or if I came across her incriminating diary somewhere and stole it. Presumably the unchristian behaviour of theft would be outweighed by the Christian act of helping keep a roof on the church. I nodded, hoping I looked more virtuous than I was feeling. Mr Thomas nodded back, still looking very solemn. My dad shot me a slightly suspicious look, said goodbye to him and took me off to say goodbye to everyone else so that we could go home for lunch.

On Sunday, after tea, I played chess with Dad. Mum was bleaching the cups, on the phone to my Nan. I knew she couldn't hear us, but I said it quietly anyway. 'Dad, will Cerys be okay?'

He nodded. 'To be honest with you, Angharad, Cerys isn't really high on my list of worries at the moment.'

I moved my knight where his queen could take it, to make him feel better. He looked at me, but I pretended to be thinking hard about my next move. He ignored my pity offering. I thought he looked tired. I was still thinking about what Jake had said. 'Dad, are the police good? Like, will they always help people in trouble?'

He looked across at me. 'Of course.'

I nodded. I wondered who I believed. He said, 'Angharad, is something worrying you?'

I shook my head. I still hadn't told him about going to Worcester tomorrow. 'How's work?' I asked.

He sighed. 'Just the same.'

That was always how work was. There wasn't exactly much crime drama. The only thing we do seem to have a few of in Llanyfenni is paedophiles and one of them was in prison anyway. And quad bike thieves. Anyway, just Llanyfenni problems.

We both watched the TV, where some programme about County Lines drug gangs was starting. My dad sighed again. 'So many problems in the world, Angharad, that could be solved with a bit of compassion and understanding.'

He reached for the remote. 'It's not exactly the sort of thing that you need to worry about, anyway.'

I moved my queen. 'Check.'

That night, before bed, I had a bath. I lay back in the hot water, looking at my legs. Bodies were so weird. Thought about Jake, wondered if he'd looked at my legs when he saw me in my nightie. Thought about lust and coveting stuff and all the other stuff the church says is bad. Stuff I'd never done before, and always wondered about. Felt like I was on a path now, and I couldn't go back, even if I wanted to.

Later that evening, I wandered downstairs to get a drink. My parents were sitting solemnly on either side of the kitchen table, instead of their usual position in front of the TV trying to remember what they'd seen every actor in before and who they used to be married to. I heard my mum. 'I have tried to talk to Marie, to get to know her, but she's so strange. I really think that girl should be in school, not roaming the streets like an alley cat.'

Ah, it was Faith. I smiled a bit to myself at the hypocrisy of my mum telling anyone off about the education of their child. I hadn't ever noticed that Faith didn't go to school. She went to dance class, which I guess I'd always thought of as pretty much the same thing.

I snuck back upstairs and lay in the dark. Faith wasn't like an alley cat, I thought. She was like a panther, all beautiful and fierce and clever.

I texted Jake to check what time we were leaving. I turned the volume up so I'd wake up when he replied. Then I lay very straight with my eyes shut hard and waited to go to sleep. It was pathetic to be so excited, as if tomorrow was Christmas.

I woke up when someone threw gravel at my window. It wasn't Jake. Which was lucky, because I looked a mess. Cerys was standing down there, in the dark, wearing a dressing gown. I could think of no reason at all why she would think this was a good time for a chat. I opened the window, reluctantly. 'Hi, Cerys.'

'Come outside,' she said, too loudly.

I don't normally swear but I was starting to understand why people did. 'For fuck's sake,' I said to myself, quietly, then put my slippers on and snuck downstairs.

Cerys was waiting outside, her hood up like some kind of elderly lady version of Yoda. 'You need to find Faith,' she said. 'I'm getting worried about her.'

I felt slightly cross. 'I'm trying!'

She looked at me dubiously. 'Are you? Or are you just hanging around with that Morgan boy?'

'He's helping! Which is more than her own mother is!'

I knew I sounded shrill and sanctimonious. Cerys nodded at me, reassuringly. 'He is,' I said again, to myself.

'Well, cariad, I don't know about that, and I wouldn't want to speak ill of someone when I might not know all the facts.'

She didn't know all of the facts. She didn't know any of the facts. Her wrinkly old hedgehog face twitched at me. 'Ah, Angharad, you look just like you used to when your mother told you that you'd had enough biscuits. Don't be angry. Just something to think about.'

I didn't know what she meant about my face, but it sounded mean. 'I am trying to find Faith,' I said, too loudly.

She nodded at me. 'Faith's a good girl,' she said, nodding at me, and I felt a weight lift off my heart.

I smiled. 'Is she?'

'And even if she isn't, not only good girls deserve a chance,' she said firmly, and tightening her dressing gown, she disappeared back into the night.

Marie

I take my pills as soon as I wake up. Make a list of what I will do. Shop. Hoover. Change the sheets. Put on the washing. Tidy away the Christmas decorations. Today will be different. And then I turn on the radio and they are talking about refugees and children dying and I realise I am crying and I wonder how everyone else can just get on with their chores when there is so much wrong with the world.

Mr Thomas says that he will pray for me.

Brad

Crack is a hurricane. Chasing the high. Fucking wonderful.

Faith

The night after the barbeque, Phil was being quiet again. There had been people in and out all day, chatting and laughing and the bank notes kept coming. Don't know why people think dealing is easy, it's hard work, talking shit and smiling, making them feel special, all mates together and the notes stacking up in a box under the table. I couldn't help thinking again about how much more we'd be making if Phil wasn't so scared of pills.

I was sitting with my feet up and a beer, staring at the cash. Phil's obsessed with Taylor Swift, so we'd had her on repeat all day. If I hadn't hated her before, I did after that. But apparently Eminen is a misogynist and not actually funny. Phil was supposed to be making tea for me and him and some girl who'd rocked up in her pyjamas. She'd gone out with him to the kitchen to 'help' and they'd been a while. I could hear her giggling.

I went to stand in the doorway. I felt like I owed Daria that much. 'Put her down and make the fucking tea, Philip.'

'Why don't you just go home?' he called back.

He sounded desperate. I laughed. When you're all in the same business, working together, you end up loving people that you wouldn't put up with normally. Like, in Llanyfenni, at the May Day carnival, we did a dance show. Halfway through the show, I didn't even hate Ella. Just for a second, until I saw her peering out over the people, hoping that Jake had turned up to see her triumph. He hadn't, obviously.

But Jed and Phil are nothing like as annoying as Ella. We were a team. I was going to miss them when I went home. And I was starting to feel like it was time to go home. See Angharad. Sort my mum out.

Maybe I could change. I tried to imagine life without weed. And vodka too, probably. And cigarettes. Swimming and dancing. Hanging out with Phil and Jed, and just drinking tea. Listening to Taylor Swift, like now, but sober. Probably going to the cinema, if I could be bothered to go to Brecon. It didn't seem natural but I was prepared to give it a go. I wondered what music Angharad listened to. Realised I was smiling to myself.

I was having some pretty warm and fuzzy positive thoughts. Which is never a good idea. I was skint but I was pretty sure some of the notes stacked up under the table would be coming my way. I'd worked for them. It did cross my mind to nick a few of them, but I wouldn't do that, not to a mate.

Phil was being quiet with me all evening. I just thought it was still about pyjama girl. I was waiting for Phil and Daria to go to bed, so I could sleep, but it was fine, I didn't mind waiting. It was their house. We were playing poker. It wasn't great. Daria insisted we listen to 'Pokerface' every five minutes and didn't know how to play, and Phil and I weren't really looking at each other, and I was trying to act like someone who didn't care if they won even though I really, really needed the fucking money.

I didn't notice at first when my phone fell out Phil's pocket. Assumed it was his. But I noticed when he got all shifty picking it up. 'Phil, why've you got my phone?'

I reached out for it. He didn't pass it over, just kind of stood there like a big tree. I waited to hear what the explanation was. 'Give me my phone,' I said, in case he had zoned out. But I knew he hadn't zoned out.

'Faith –'

Phil was trying to look like he didn't give a shit, but I know him too well. He was scared. I was fuming. He was looking everywhere but not at me. The hair on my arms were standing up, like they knew I was in trouble before I did. He was rubbing his hand on his cheek, which would have been cute if he was a kid. 'I wish you hadn't come,' he said slowly.

'You said to come here. It was your idea.'

'Jamie's idea.'

I stared at him. Of course it was. 'Why?'

Phil was tapping his fingers on his palm. He got a cigarette out. I felt my chest getting tight. 'Why, Phil?'

'I told you to go back. You should have gone back.'

I was less angry now and more freaked out. Phil still hadn't lit the cigarette, was tapping that now, still not looking at me. Then he dropped his head down onto his hands. His fingers were over his eyes. Like if he couldn't see me, I wasn't there. I stood up. I wanted to ask what was going on, why he was being so strange, but I also really, really didn't want to know. 'Are you going to give me my phone?'

My voice wasn't shaking. It's not like it's the first time I've been screwed over. The important thing is just to get through it. You don't need to let them see if you care. Phil still wouldn't look at me. Daria was watching, mouth open. I blew her a kiss. 'Your boyfriend's screwing other women. You can do better than him.'

She looked doubtful. I walked out into the street and didn't look back till I heard the door shut. I didn't want to go to fucking sweaty Jed's but if it was there or a long walk and then sitting on some bench at the station till the morning, then I chose Jed's. I couldn't text him to tell him I was coming, obviously. What with not having a phone. Thinking about the phone reminded me that I didn't have any money yet either. Dicks.

The air was warm. I walked along the river. In winter, when there's more water, you see old trees and cows all blown up like balloons and loads of torn plastic getting washed down. Now, there's barely any water but you can see the mud in the street lights and it stinks. I climbed through the barrier at the lock and looked down. Water was trickling out into the mud way, way below. I wondered how long you would take to sink into it, if you jumped.

Jed wasn't surprised to see me. He had music on too loud, and the place stank of weed and looked a state. When he looked at me, his eyes kind of slid away. He just pointed to a sofa and handed me a can. I didn't take my coat off. It was cold, and I was so tired. And I wanted to keep as many layers between me and his sweated-on settee as I could. 'What's up, Jed?'

He finally looked at me. His knee was jiggling up and down. His eyes were tired. I felt weirdly sorry for him. He stared for ages before he spoke, but that wasn't exactly unusual for him. 'Faith —' he said.

We waited to see if there was any more explanation. He shut his eyes and tipped his head back. 'Oh, Faith.'

Brilliant. I could feel my eyes closing and had to force myself to open them again. I put the can down. I felt sick, not like me. Jed muttered something I couldn't make out, opened his eyes and looked at me, shaking his head.

I woke up a bit later when he sat down next to me. I was awake, but I kept my eyes shut. I've been here before. I know the score. 'Faith?' he said quietly, again.

I knew what he wanted. What they all want. Dicks. They're all dicks. I could feel him moving about next to me. Hoped he wasn't getting his cock out. I kept my eyes shut, didn't move, didn't think about any of it. Stayed quiet and still and thought about Angharad, sitting in silence against the church wall, waiting for the butterflies.

Mr Thomas

Everyone is welcome at Llanyfenni Parish Church. Whatever sins they have committed, we will always welcome them. There was no reason for the rumours about Mrs Jones – Ms Jones as she's calling herself now. She would have been just as welcome to remain in the congregation as Mr Jones. I wouldn't encourage anyone to take sides, or to sit in judgement because that is for the Lord. I hear now that she goes to the chapel out on the Llangadog road, and I pray for her, and hope for her salvation.

Faith

Brad rocked up at Jed's around four in the morning. I'm guessing, because obviously I didn't have my fucking phone.

Jed had got bored of whispering my name at me after a bit and fucked off. Which was good, waking up was crap enough without being covered in sweaty jizz. Then the next thing I knew the birds were singing and there was a strong smell of expensive aftershave and Brad was standing just inside the door. Jed came downstairs, yawning. 'Fucking hell,' he grumbled.

He didn't say anything else because Brad whacked him across the face. Jed stepped back, blood trickling down from his nose. He stood there, looking pathetic, holding it.

My eyes were open, but I was in no mood to get involved in Jed's business so I just lay and watched the entertainment. It didn't last long. I was wrong to think this was about Jed. It turned out to be about me.

Brad looked down and I looked up, into his big brown eyes. To be fair, wearing a jacket so you couldn't see his ridiculous muscles, Brad was quite sexy. It was a shame he was a man, and possibly a bit of a psychopath. 'Faith,' he said.

Maybe my life was just going to be men saying my name now and then groping me. Maybe I was dead and this was hell. I sat up.

Brad sat down next to me, carefully, like I was a kitten. Like a social worker does when they're about to say something grim like, 'Your little brother's being taken into care,' or 'Your mother hasn't been taking her medication and we have taken her back to hospital'. I wanted to tell him that he didn't need to be careful around me, I wasn't a kitten and I had probably heard worse.

But it wasn't bad news. 'I know Jed's a mate of yours,' Brad said, and then stopped.

After spending some of the night wondering if I was going to have Jed's cock shoved in my face, and the way that Jed was sitting sadly in a corner still clutching his nose, I wasn't exactly feeling that.

'I hate him.' I made sure I was loud enough for him to hear. 'He's a sweaty cunt,' I said.

Brad was nodding, fast, and looking kind of sad but manly. 'I trusted him, Faith, and I'm pretty pissed off that he's let me down.'

I raised my eyebrows. 'No shit.'

As soon as I said it I realised I should have kept quiet, but Brad was laughing. Pretty loudly for 4am but at least he was cheery. 'Yeah, well, I've got a bit of a temper. It's not the first time me and Jed have fallen out.'

I remembered poor, pathetic Jed, shaking and sweating at Phil's. I thought about defending Jed. Then I thought about him sitting next to me on the settee whispering my name and I didn't bother standing up for him. 'I don't want you to think I just go around hurting people.' Brad grinned at me again. 'It's not what it looks like.'

I shouldn't have laughed, with Jed crying and bleeding. Maybe I was a bit hysterical. Brad laughed too. After we had finished cackling, he got up. 'I'll put the kettle on, and then maybe you and me can have a chat?'

I took out a cigarette. Four left in the packet. I heard Brad fill the kettle, and then open the door out onto the balcony. I lit up. I offered Jed one because I'm not a bad person, but he was still busy crying. There was snot and blood on his chin, but I figured he'd be alright. It didn't look broken.

I was more worried about myself. Four cigarettes, about three quid in my pocket and no phone. I wondered if Jed had any cash lying around. Phil owed me. I needed it if I was going to get home. I wasn't that fussed about the Llanyfenni train, I could just tell them a story about my sick nan or something, but they wouldn't let me through the barriers at Worcester without a ticket. They have police at Worcester sometimes now.

When Brad came back in, grinning even more, Jed ran out of the room looking sick. Brad rolled his eyes at him and stuck a mug in my hand. He'd put about a million sugars in it, which was what I needed. 'I'm sorry Jed and Phil messed you around,' Brad said.

'Phil took my phone.'

'Confession time.' He was grinning again, as if we were both going to find this funny. 'I told them to get rid of your phone.'

'Nice one. Thanks, Brad.'

He stopped smiling. 'Can I explain?'

I shrugged. It all seemed a bit pointless, him explaining. 'Come on, Faith, I like you. We're two of a kind.'

Brilliant, I thought. Finally I meet a kindred spirit and he smells of Lynx and Armani, sells coke and steals phones. I just looked at him. First rule with men. Act dumb. Say nothing. First two rules. 'You're smarter than that, Faith. Right, I've brought biscuits. Sit there, drink your tea, and I'll tell you what's happening.'

And he fished a packet of hobnobs out his jacket pocket, tore them open and stuck them in front of me. I was pretty hungry and hobnobs are lush, so I sat and listened. I was impressed. What sort of man carries emergency hobnobs?

'So me and Jamie, we're good at what we do. Bit of weed, pills, some brown but mainly crack. Do you know about crack?'

I shrugged. I only knew what everyone else knew. You made a shitload of money selling it, people loved it, and it seemed to involve getting knifed a bit sometimes. 'Lush stuff. Me and Jamie, we want to make a lot of dollars with the crack. But we're too big for Bristol now, so we've been expanding.'

'Like Aldi and Lidl?' I said, just to piss him off.

'No, Faith, not really.'

'Too big for Bristol?' I asked.

That seemed unlikely. How could you be too big for Bristol? Too scared for Bristol, I reckoned. He just ignored the question and carried on talking. 'At first, just a few sellers here, but now we've loads. Good people. Clever people who understand the game.'

I wasn't sure how Phil and Jed fit in. 'Wow.'

'But, the thing is, Phil and Jed just ain't cutting it.'

No shit. I tried to look surprised and disappointed.

Brad shrugged, slurped his tea. He was breathing fast, getting twitchy again. 'They're fucking useless, Faith.'

I couldn't argue with that. They were fucking useless. 'Eat the hobnobs,' Brad said.

I kept eating. I love hobnobs. Brad kept talking. 'I get that they're hippies, I'm not judging them. I know loads of hippies. I'm not asking them to sell the crack if they don't want to. They don't even have to sell the coke, I admire them for having principals. It's a bit gutting because most hippies love the coke, but it is how it is. I don't beg, I have a load of people who'd love the chance to sell crack. It's good stuff. People are usually begging me. I don't care about the crack or the coke.'

I feel sick again. Too many hobnobs. I wondered when I'd get a chance to brush my teeth. Brad was still banging on. 'But they're fucking useless. They've got no ambition, and that really pisses me off. They want the money, but they're not doing the work.'

I thought sadly about how much I loved the money too. Brad nodded. 'We all love the dollars, Faith. Make no mistake about it, there's a lot of dollars, especially with the crack. But you have to put in the effort. I don't mind helping people get started, me and Jamie want to help, but you have to let yourself be helped. Those boys wanted none of the work. And that's just taking advantage, Faith.'

He looked at me, hands held up. 'What can you do?' I said.

He nodded. 'That's it, Faith. They can't have it all the ways. And I couldn't stand watching them messing you about. You're a bright girl, you know the score, and you're good at it. You've been doing really well in Llanyfenni. Really well.'

'I am pretty good.' I agreed.

I was. Before me, Llanyfenni just had Donovan. And Scary Sarah if you wanted coke, but she was really scary. I'm like

Llanyfenni's Amazon of weed. Reliable, door-to-door service. But with a smile and no hassling to pay more for Prime. It was all Prime, with me.

'And they were just messing you about, letting you sit around in Worcester and work for them and I bet they didn't even give you any of the dollar.'

I really wished he'd stop saying dollar. And they hadn't exactly been letting me sit around in Worcester. I'd worked hard. I didn't tell Brad that Phil had told me to go home at least once, and I'd ignored him.

Brad shrugged with his hands turned up again. 'They're just messing you around, Faith. Taking advantage of you, and taking advantage of me. Like we're proper mugs. Now, you're like me, you understand the business, you understand the people. And you're hungry.'

The hobnob packet was empty. He saw me looking. 'Not hungry for food, Faith, hungry for dollars.'

'Lend us a tenner?'

I thought it was worth a try. Brad laughed. 'Funny girl.'

I still wasn't laughing. He carried on. 'So what I reckon is that we cut out the middle guys, and you just come straight to me. Like Phil and Jed do. But on better terms because you're not a useless fuckwit. Just buy from me and save yourself a bit of extra cash. And we'll figure out some great places to sell. You don't need to be stuck in that Welsh shithole.'

'I like Llanyfenni.'

He got out his wallet, rammed full of notes. We both looked at them and he laughed loudly again. 'Look! I'm just walking around with all this cash on me and people are giving it to me faster than I can spend it.'

He pulled a card out of the wallet. It was a business card, with a number and a picture of a swan. Nothing else. 'It's classy,' Brad said. 'I designed it myself. You can have a new phone, I'll give you one, with this number, and I can help you get the business. Easier for you. And you can hand these out. All professional.'

I looked at the swan, imagined myself giving one to Jake and Ella and the rest of them in Llanyfenni. Wasn't sure if I would look cool or just ridiculous. I handed the card back and Brad tucked it away. 'Let me take you out for breakfast, Faith. It's been a rough night for you and some of that's my fault. Phil isn't the sharpest. This is exactly the sort of thing I'm talking about though, you see what I mean. Bloody nightmare. Wait here.'

He wandered back out onto the balcony and I waited. I could hear Jed moving about upstairs. Thought about saying goodbye. Decided not to.

It was already light as we walked to Brad's car. Sunrise, handsome bloke, gorgeous girl, flash car. The air was warm and a bit breezy. I wondered when I could get hold of some of Brad's dollars.

He drove a black BMW, obviously, because he was a crack dealer. The seats were leather. 'Easier to wash the blood and that off,' Brad said and laughed.

'Ha.'

'Only joking with you, babe. But also, worth thinking about. When you're buying your own.'

I wondered how you got to be someone who factored that in. Fuel economy, engine size, wipe clean seats. 'I'm fifteen, Brad.'

'Well, stick with me, it won't be long. Time will fly, when you're having fun. And fifteen? Really?'

I nodded. He looked at my face, and then down at my tits. 'Cool. Fifteen. Wild. Get in the car.'

I got in. I hate leather. It smells of cow and it feels weird. Lynx and dead cow filling up my nose. Awesome.

I wondered if I should try and be less negative. Maybe if I smiled more, bad stuff would stop happening. I was pretty sure I'd seen a photo of me smiling when I was a toddler. Maybe I could get back in the habit.

The cafe was shite. For no apparent reason, except so that Brad could drive like a prick, we'd had to drive down the M5 to some transport cafe. There were a couple of lorries parked up outside and a couple of lorry-driver types sitting, separately, at tables inside. One was a woman. She wasn't my type, but I smiled at her anyway. Practising. She smiled back.

I wondered if this was a sign that my life was changing for the better. Maybe the nice lorry lady and I would drive off somewhere together. Somewhere far away. Or maybe she would ask me if I was alright, take me to the train, buy me a ticket.

As we sat down, my future wife got up and walked out the door. I watched her go. As she passed our table she winked at me. Or maybe just blinked, I could only see one side of her face.

Brad was watching me. 'So Phil says you only fancy girls?' Brad asked.

'Mmm,' I said, just to keep the conversation going.

He laughed again. 'Well, no need to worry about that now. Shall we talk business?'

It turned out that it wasn't really talking business so much as Brad explaining to me lots of times in different ways how much dollar I would make without Jed and Phil holding me back, travelling about the country selling crack. He made it sound like a holiday. I had a Full English and three cups of tea and then a coffee. Thought about Angharad and her beautiful blue eyes and funny dresses and what might happen when I saw her again.

Angharad

Jake didn't turn up at the station. Maybe he never meant to.

I had got to the station ten minutes early. The train was due at 6.28am. Which was early, but made it feel like a proper adventure. There were a couple of other people waiting. No sign of Jake yet. I'd brought a small rucksack with a packed lunch and some snacks for the train. I hadn't been on a train for a long time, so I'd brought a flask of coffee because I wasn't sure if there would be any. Drinking coffee would look cool and make it very clear that I wasn't a child.

It was cold waiting on the platform even though I'd brought a hoodie. I had thought about bringing my waterproof coat. The sun had barely stopped shining for weeks, it was bound to at some point. But it didn't seem very sophisticated. And the way that people laughed at Wales for being so rainy made it sound like England was less rainy. Though it was mainly the sophisticated thing.

I had been awake since about 3am. I had washed my hair in the sink, so mum wouldn't hear the shower. I'd put mascara on, and lipstick, and then wiped it off again. I'd tried on different outfits and tiptoed out to look at myself in the bathroom mirror. I'm not allowed a mirror, because vanity is a sin (my mum) and for my mental health (my dad). We only have a tiny one in the bathroom, so that we can make sure that we're brushing our teeth properly, and not going out covered in toothpaste. It's not great, if you are going on a sort of date with a hot Morgan brother. I ended up just wearing my jeans. My unfashionable jeans, because I'm not allowed in New Look, or anywhere that sells cheap, normal clothes which is apparently throwaway fashion (my dad). In books, teenagers who just shop in charity shops look different in a quirky, cool way. Llanyfenni doesn't have those sorts of charity shops.

I knew my jeans were embarrassing, so I tried to make up for them by wearing a vest top that I'm not normally allowed out in unless it's covered up by something else. Because of modesty (my mum). My boobs were falling out a bit, but I figured Jake probably liked that. I still looked less of a slut than Ella, anyway. I tied my hair up and then took it back down.

Before I got to the station, I had been a bit worried about knowing where to stand, but there were screens telling you which side of the track went in which direction. We had to change in Hereford.

I started getting worried about two minutes later. What if Jake missed the train? What if he'd slept in? I held my phone in my hand, really wanting to text him, just to make sure, and knowing I was being irrational. When I heard the train, my chest went tight.

It stopped next to me and Jake didn't come running up. So I got on the train. There was only one carriage. I sat by the window, telling myself I wasn't really committed because I could just get off at the next stop and come back. Even if I had to wait. Though the next couple of stops turned out to be tiny request stops and then the conductor came and I bought a return ticket just in case I did want to go all the way and then by the time we got to a proper station I felt like I had committed, at least as far as Hereford.

I ended up quite enjoying the first train. I sat and drank my coffee. Not having Jake meant that I could have another cup on the next train. My stomach was aching, and I wasn't sure if it was because I was hungry or scared. I couldn't believe that Jake had forgotten, and was hoping that he might be waking up now and panicking, rushing to get the next train. Or even to put on his sexy leathers and drive up on his bike to meet me on the platform in Hereford, or even Worcester.

I finished the coffee. If Jake wasn't waking up and he wasn't coming with me then I would have to find Phil myself and I didn't know where he lived. I needed to get his number, so in the end I texted Jake. I made sure that I didn't sound grumpy in case that meant that he didn't answer. But he didn't answer anyway.

I sat back and looked out of the window. It was another gorgeous day. It didn't feel like anything bad could happen. So I called him. I called him four times before he answered. I didn't mean to keep phoning, but I couldn't help myself. I wasn't sure whether he'd be angry, but he sounded hardly awake. 'Oh shit, babe! Please tell me you're not on the train.'

'Yeah, but it's fine, don't worry.'

I didn't want him to feel bad. 'Could you give me Phil's number?'

'Are you pissed off? I didn't think you'd actually go! You're nuts.'

I was pissed off with both of us. Pissed off with him for not coming and pissed off with myself for even thinking that he was going to come. For spending so long worrying about my jeans. For imagining him waiting for me at Hereford. 'No, I'm not pissed off. I thought we were going, but you didn't come, so I just got the train myself.'

'Oh, Angh! By yourself? Shit, man, I'm sorry.'

'It's okay, I have been on a train before.'

I was too proud to tell him it was with my mum. He was quiet for a second. 'Angh, are you crying? Shit, don't cry!'

'I just thought we'd do it together. I brought coffee for you.'

'Oh, you little sweetie. I should have realised. My fault. I'm sorry.'

I snuffled into the phone a bit. Like an idiot. 'Please, Angh, don't cry. I promise I'll take you out. Make it up to you. Tomorrow? You could tell me all about it? You being brave in the city?'

I thought about that. Wiped my nose with my hand and hoped he hadn't heard. He sighed. 'I really am sorry. I should have known you were serious. And you are definitely doing the right thing. I know I've been a bit shit the last few days. Call me any time if you need me. Don't worry about Ella. None of that's your problem. Are you okay?'

'I'm okay.'

'Good girl! I can't believe you're doing this. I have to be honest, when I first met you, I thought you were a bit weird but you're amazing! I'll send Phil's number.'

'Jake, is Phil selling drugs too?'

'Just weed, so you don't need to worry, Princess.'

He ended the call. He sent the number through. He called back a minute later. 'Did you get it, babe?'

'Yes, thanks.'

'Brilliant! Listen, Angh – call me if you need me today. I mean it.'

'Okay.'

There was a moment's silence. 'Okay. Bye, then, Angharad.'

I kept listening, in case he said anything else, but he just ended the call. I still didn't know how to get Phil's address, especially if Faith had told him that she hated me. I decided to text. 'Hi. I got your number from a guy in Wales, can I come round?'

I thought about Marie giving Jake a phone number to buy weed. Even though she was a mum. I wondered if I was the only person in Llanyfenni who wasn't interested in drugs.

It seemed more likely that Phil would give me his address if he thought I was a customer than because I was the person Faith was trying to avoid. And someone that bought weed probably wouldn't be texting at 7am. I would wait until I got to Worcester.

I wondered if all that chess was turning out to be useful. Maybe more useful than the police genes. I was a bit doubtful about them when I thought about my dad.

I was pretty smug on the first train. The accidental kiss in the park could have happened to anyone, but if I had upset Faith, then I was going to sort it out. I had impressed Jake Morgan. And shown my parents that I wasn't a toddler. And it was fun, trundling along the mountainsides in a tiny train.

An avenging angel, going to rescue a fallen lamb from a den of sin. And hopefully Faith would be sitting on Phil's sofa and would be pleased to see me and not completely freaked out that I'd followed her to England. Even the kiss seemed quite cool now I was sitting on the train thinking about it. And maybe my jeans wouldn't be so embarrassing in Worcester.

I managed the change at Hereford. It wasn't too bad, and I had half an hour. I was falling asleep by the time we were getting close to Worcester. I'd been there before, but in the car with my mum, on the way to a festival. A Christian festival. We didn't stay long at the festival. It was all a bit busy for quiet Christians like us, and there were some teenagers who definitely seemed drunk. On our way to the festival, we had stopped at a farm shop and bought some pasties and fruit. There were bouncy castles and big inflatable slides behind the farmhouse. Worcester seemed fun, I'd thought. But as the train went past rows and rows of brick houses and warehouses it felt different altogether.

Marie, Llanyfenni

In the afternoons, I watch Finding Nemo. Wait to see if Faith comes home. Or Jake comes round again. It would be nice to have a visitor.

Faith

After the breakfast, Brad disappeared again into some bushes while I went for a pee. I wondered what exactly he was on that seemed to take up so much time. He drove even faster back, turning to grin at me every so often. 'Scared?'

'I don't scare easy,' I said.

Blokes like it when you say that kind of thing. He had big hands. Very big hands. 'I love your attitude, babe.'

I nodded and smiled. 'Do you mind dropping me at the station?'

'Yeah, yeah, sure. Or come to Jamie's for a bit? You'll like it, I reckon, it's lush. I can give you some more stuff to sell too. Talk about the plan. Where's best for you to go next? Do you want to borrow some cash?' He laughed again.

I didn't laugh, but I was pleased we seemed on the same page about the money. If I had to make him happy by going to Jamie's, then I'd make him happy by going to Jamie's.

Brad was right, Jamie's was awesome. Brad parked his ridiculous car in some back street, and I was thinking that this was literally the uncoolest place to live ever, but then he winked at me and took my hand. I hate holding hands with people. Apart from Angharad, she had very nice, squidgy hands. But Brad's massive hand was all over mine and he was pulling me along. I was pretty sure if he squeezed any harder he was going to break a bone. He probably wouldn't even notice.

Jamie's boat was huge, all metal and black and rust and big windows with bars on. There was a name painted on the back. Journey's End, in white, messy letters, like someone high had painted them for a laugh. I thought boats were called things like Morning Star and Meander. And I'd never seen anything like it on the canal before. Brad winked at me. 'Come on, babe.'

We sat on the roof, which Jamie kept calling the deck, like it was a yacht, and Jamie brought up sausages and Brad told me how cool I was and how much they liked me and how much fun we were going to have. The canal was still, with ducks bobbing about. It was weirdly private. Brad kept grinning at me. I couldn't help grinning back. He was right, it was really lush. He passed me a warm bottle of beer. 'Cheers,' he said, and we all clinked bottles.

Angharad

It was just after nine when I arrived in Worcester. I managed to get out of the station and kept walking until I saw a Costa. I headed straight for it. The people had accents like Faith and Marie's, which I guess wasn't surprising, but it felt weird. There were women in headscarves, and women with shaved heads and women in tiny skirts with everything hanging out. It wasn't as busy as I'd imagined. It was okay, I coped. I could sort of see that it would be a bit exciting, if you got used to it.

There was a little shop, selling fruit that I had never seen before. Signs stuck in the window in languages I didn't know. There were people in doorways sitting, begging for money, like on the news. I gave a woman with a dog one of my tenners and then felt guilty about keeping the other. Christians are supposed to give, if they have two coats, they should give one away, maybe even both if someone needs them. But I didn't want to give away my money. I could see that being good must be more complicated in Worcester.

I texted Jake, to tell him I had arrived. He replied a few minutes later, 'Well done u rock'.

I wished he punctuated texts properly, it didn't take any longer and it made everything a lot easier to understand. I joined the queue. Nothing scary was happening. I tried to ignore the voice in my brain which kept saying 'Nothing scary *yet*.'

Brad

When Jamie said we needed cute girls to move stuff up country for us, I argued. I thought the cute girls would be too up themselves to help us out. But Faith understands me. If I had a girl like Faith, I think I could be okay. Like a normal person. Jamie says normal people don't smoke rocks. But I could change. Faith could help me.

Jamie

Paul drinks in my local. He's a sad old boy. I buy him a drink now and again and he tells me about his life. It's what you'd expect – woman who didn't understand him, kids who don't want to know, holding on to a job by the skin of his teeth. Every time I see him, it reminds me of why I'm doing this. I don't want to be Paul.

I was thinking about Paul while I waited for Brad to appear with Faith. I was starting to think that the cute girl thing was a mistake. Sourcing a few, as a kind of test run, hadn't turned out to be as hard as I'd thought but letting Brad near them was definitely a mistake. As if I didn't have enough to do.

Angharad

I text Phil just before ten, when the girl behind the counter was starting to look pissed off with me. He didn't seem suspicious, just sent a postcode, and a house number. I guessed that must be what it was anyway. I wondered if that was the sort of thing that happened to him all the time, people just turning up at his house. Maybe even when he was having his dinner.

I ignored the counter girl for another few minutes while I put the postcode into Google maps. Broadway. That sounded fairly cheery, I thought. I noticed my battery was at seventy per cent already. I decided to figure out the buses there and back now, and write them down, just in case.

The bus drove out through the city. So many people. And they all seemed very unfriendly. Not mean, just as if they didn't care at all about me. I kept watching the little blue dot on my phone as we travelled along.

The bus stop was on a huge road but I knew the house was near the canal and a park. It turned out to be a strange, modern housing estate jammed in the middle of an industrial estate. I added it to my list of the sorts of places you could buy drugs that weren't scary flats. Wished I was at home learning about atoms, instead of here, learning about the accommodation choices of dodgy men.

Faith

Inside the boat, there were candles, and beanbags and comfy chairs with blinds over the massive barred windows and soft music. Jamie headed through a door, I could hear him humming to himself and moving about. I leaned against the door frame. 'Woah, it's got a real kitchen and everything!'

'Galley,' Jamie said pissily. 'On a boat, it's a galley.'

Brad rolled his eyes at me. 'Go in and see what he's doing.'

Jamie was pretending to be such a cool dude that he wasn't paying any attention to me, so I hopped up on the counter beside him to see better. He had a massive bag of coke, which was pretty cool. And baking powder. There was a crate of lager on the side so I helped myself to another one. I tipped a bit down my throat and thought about how awesome I probably looked right now. If anyone could see me. Angharad, for example. Though maybe she wouldn't be that impressed by me drinking while I watched some dodgy Bristol geezer making crack. On a boat though. Surely she'd be impressed by the boat. 'Are you watching?' Jamie asked.

'Yeah, yeah, totally.'

He was stirring something in a jar. 'So this is coke, really good stuff.'

I nodded, to show willing. A surprising amount of listening to annoying men explaining things seems to be involved with the dealing. 'And what are you mixing it with?' I asked, trying to look like I cared.

Jamie looked a bit suspicious. 'Water. Look, Faith, are you interested, or not?'

Brad had appeared in the doorway. 'She's interested.'

I raised my eyebrows at him. 'How much did you say you were selling this for?'

Brad pointed at a bucket in the corner. It was filled with cash, notes and coins, heaped up to the top. I tried to look unimpressed. Brad walked across the kitchen – galley – and opened a cupboard door. There were three more buckets in there, money spilling out the top. 'That's just change, Faith.'

'Slush fund,' Jamie agreed, without looking away from whatever weird mixture he was cooking.

'A lot of dollar,' Brad nodded.

'Thousand pounds a day you can get, down in Bristol.'

I swigged my beer. Most of my life, I couldn't buy chewing gum, chocolate, anything really. It wasn't like my mum had been handing out pocket money. And now I had cigarettes, warm coat, phone. Not a phone, I remembered. No phone – no actual money in my pocket, last pack of ciggies. But all that cash, lying there, giving me hope.

'You wanna try?' Brad held out a bag.

Angharad

Like a baby, I called Jake. He answered straight away. I could hear garage noises in the background. At least he was at work, and not with Ella. 'Are you okay? I've been thinking, Angh, I don't think I should have let you go alone. Where are you?'

'Down the road from Phil's.'

'I don't think you should go there. What if he was lying and he's killed Faith and fed her to the pigs?'

I swallowed. 'I don't think they have pigs here. But thanks, Jake.'

He sounded a bit panicked. 'Or in the canal. There's a canal in Worcester. A big one. And a park. People get raped and stabbed in cities all the time.'

'Jake, stop looking at the internet.'

'Just stay away from the park.'

'I'm by a park right now. And the canal.'

'Fuck's sake, Angharad, get away from it then! What if they push you in?'

I walked back towards the road. Feeling irritated by Jake was definitely making me feel less nervous. 'You told me to come! You were supposed to be here!'

'Yeah, yeah, I know, Sweetie.'

'I can't just go back now. I had to get two trains and a bus. What if Faith's just sitting watching telly?'

'Then why doesn't she answer her phone?'

'Jake!' My throat was tight again. 'I said that! You said it was alright. What am I supposed to do now?'

I stared off down the street, towards the house. It all looked peaceful enough. A door opened and a girl came out. I couldn't see which house she'd come from. I took a deep breath. 'Hang on, Jake.'

'What? Babe, where are you going?'

I ended the call and put my phone in my pocket, and

walked towards her. She was tiny, and not much older than me. She had a huge red hair clip on, bouncing around as she walked, and a skirt even shorter than Faith's. She looked a bit like a Barbie doll, but with dreadlocked hair. Twitter is rude about white people with dreadlocks but that made me feel more confident. I stopped in front of her. It was obvious I wanted to talk to her, there was no one else around. 'Excuse me?'

She looked startled. 'Yeah? What's up?'

'I'm looking for 274. Phil's house.'

She squinted her eyes at me suspiciously. 'Back there,' she pointed with her thumb.

'The thing is, I'm trying to find my friend. Faith. She was staying there. Did you see her?'

She was jiggling away, restlessly. I could see her bra underneath her tiny top. I wondered if it was because I'd kissed a girl that I was noticing girl's underwear more. Or maybe it was the new company I was keeping. I didn't remember ever being interested in any of the Home Ed girls' underwear. She was grinning at me. 'You're a friend of Faith's? Little Faith? Went to Wales? Cocky little cow?'

I felt a huge relief. She was safe. Coming here had been an over-reaction. 'Thank you, God,' I thought.

'Yes!' I decided not to explain that the whole friend thing was complicated. 'Is she there?'

'Not now she's not.'

She had stopped smiling and looked suddenly older, like an adult. 'Maybe I'll catch her later then,' I said.

I still hadn't figured out if I wanted to be face to face with Faith. 'Friend or girlfriend?' she asked.

I felt myself blush and she laughed. I said, 'I might have upset her.'

'Me too.' She nodded. 'Come with me.'

She headed off down towards the path by the canal. I followed her. We sat on the edge of the path, with our legs hanging over the canal. You could hear birds singing and there was a swan and trees hanging over on the other side. There was a lot of litter floating down the canal. It wasn't like an Instagram photo or anything. We sat for a minute, then she started jiggling again.

She took my hand. 'I don't want to upset you, Blondie, but there's stuff you should know.'

She stared into my eyes. It felt a bit intense, but I didn't want to offend her by looking away. 'What is it?' I asked when it felt like the staring had gone on long enough.

'I don't know if Faith is cheating on you. I'm sorry to tell you, because I know it hurts.'

'Oh.'

I had a lot of questions, but I kept them to myself. The girl kept talking. 'She's a liar and she didn't tell me the truth about Phil and I thought she was my friend. I don't want to lie to you. Spiritually, it's not cool.'

I agreed with that. She said, 'I don't want to be like her.'

'What did she do?'

The girl looked sad. She took my hand. 'She tried to kiss me. Behind Phil's back.'

Something about that seemed unlikely, but what did I know? 'Where is she now?'

'Thank you for not being angry with me. I am totally sorry. Phil and Faith, they're not good people.'

'Is she okay though?'

'I've tried to help him. But I'm not sure he wants to change.' She stared out across the canal. 'You have to want to change, do you know what I mean?'

I nodded, relieved she'd stopped staring at me and finally I could blink without feeling rude. I was trying to absorb that Faith might have just disappeared on me again. After possibly kissing this dreadlocked girl.

'Even moving her in with us, it's not on, without asking me.'

'So Faith was staying with you and Phil?'

I felt better that she'd been with a couple, even if this girl seemed a bit odd. And to have weird ideas about personal space. The girl nodded. 'I love him. Wish I didn't. He doesn't bring me anything but pain. But I'll leave in the end. Some guys are going to help me.'

I didn't feel like I was making much progress. I tried to think like a chess player and sneak up on her. Conversationally, not physically. 'When did you last see her?'

'I hope she didn't use my toothbrush. I hate that.'

I tried not to think about Faith using this girl's toothbrush. Kissing her. The girl was still talking. 'She didn't do bugger all around the house, just sat round, rolling spliffs and making him laugh.'

She was looking at me intently, as if she was trying to judge my reaction. 'And then she came on to me.'

The girl was still holding my hand. I wondered if this would turn out to be like Ella's story about Faith going away with Jake. I couldn't imagine people gossiping about me like that. It was starting to feel pretty sweaty, but it seemed rude to let go. She was blushing, but delicately, like a china doll. She looked down, and nodded, looking shy.

I carried on with the questions. 'And after that Faith went away?'

'Well, after a bit.'

I wondered if that was just what Faith did. Travelled around the country kissing girls, making them feel special, and then abandoning them. I wished I knew her better. 'Where did she go?'

She shrugged. ' Maybe Jed's. Last night. So me and Phil, we're back to how we were before now. He's not gonna change. And I just can't live like this.'

'Where will you go?'

'I dunno, Blondie. Been with him since I was fourteen.

But there's these guys, they might help me out.' She looked worried. 'They might, but I owe them though, I owe them already, so I dunno.'

I didn't let myself get side-tracked. 'I need to find Faith.'

'Well, you can't call her. Phil and Jed took her phone. And Phil won't tell me why. He won't even tell me why, and that's not right. When you love someone, you should tell them things.' Her face was worried. 'You should tell them things, even the bad things. Do you think, Blondie? You should tell them everything?'

I thought. Ignored what the church would say and thought about real life. Remembered sitting with Faith, with her telling me snippets about her life and none of the important stuff. Thought about Jake, and Ella. And thought about all the lies I had told since I met Faith. Thought about God and my pure heart tarnishing with every bad thing I did. 'I think it's better not to lie,' I said. I didn't mention the heart tarnishing theory,

She nodded sadly. 'He's going be so angry.'

'He sounds a bit scary?'

'He is a bit. You know what men are like.'

'Why did he take her phone?'

'That's what I'm saying. You're just a kid. You need to be careful. Some of the men, Brad and that Jamie, they're not playing around.'

I nodded, as if I had any idea what she was talking about. 'But do you know where she is now?'

'No. Maybe on the Journey's End in town. That's where they go. I think Jamie's a Scorpio. Very passionate.'

'Journey's End?'

'Yeah. Listen, I better go and tell Phil you were here. He's at home waiting for some girl.'

She stared at me, looking suddenly suspicious. 'Is it you?'

I kept quiet. 'Bloody hell!' She sounded a bit admiring. 'You better go. They'll freak out if they think someone's sniffing round after Faith. Just stay away.'

She let go of my hand and stood up, so I did too. 'You should run away. They're gonna be so angry.'

She was backing away. I could see the whites of her eyes, looking huge. I felt scared too. 'Don't tell them!' I said firmly. 'Don't tell them and they won't know.'

'I can't! You said to tell the truth. I want to tell Phil everything. Because I love him. I told you. I mustn't keep secrets. What if he says 'where were you?' – what am I supposed to say? I won't be able to help myself. And they'll go nuts. You should get out of here.'

My heart was beating hard again. I couldn't help remembering Jake panicking that I'd get killed.

I did what she said, and ran, as fast as I could, down the path and up to the main road. People were looking at me, running in my embarrassing jeans, in the middle of the day, but I was too scared to stop.

I was running along the side of the road, along where the bus had come, and as soon as I saw a bus stop with other people at it I ran straight towards it. I could feel my face burning hot. My chest was tight. Once I stopped I could feel the sweat dripping down me. My hands started shaking, so I put them in my pockets. 'I'm safe. I'm safe,' I told myself again and again, and hoped it was true.

Surely it was true. The girl seemed really confused and I didn't see what the problem was with wanting to see Faith. I just wanted to check that she was okay. Though it was starting to feel like maybe she wasn't. I didn't have a plan for that. I was fifteen, a long way from home and I was very scared. There were two old ladies at the bus stop and they looked carefully away from me until the bus came.

Jamie

It's easy, what we do. It's still work, cooking and wrapping and packing. And now organising the girls, but if that gets too much I have a few ideas about what we can do with them.

I don't have to be at home in some shitty flat with black on the walls that comes back even if you scrub real hard and everything always feeling wet, and lifts that stink of piss. And we're fucking doing it, we're making money and sorting ourselves out, and we've got the car and the flats and the girls. Even if they are scummy ones. But that'll change, I can feel it, and one day there'll be good girls, clean girls with long blonde pony tails and nice little cunts that everyone hasn't been up and they'll be begging us. That's the dream, anyway.

Faith

Obviously I said no to the crack. That was a no-brainer. But I was starting to wonder why I was there. Like, why they wanted me there. We were sitting wrapping up little packets of crack. Brad and Jamie were much faster than me. 'You're pretty good at this,' Brad said.

'You need to use less foil, you're wasting it,' Jamie told me.

I was doing my best. I'm not exactly an experienced crack wrapper. Or any kind of wrapping, my mum wasn't big on presents. Or Christmas. Last year, I'd bought her some chocolates from B&M. I had bigger plans for this year. Now it was easy to start thinking about the buckets of cash and the kind of presents you could buy with them. I bet Brad got his mum some nice Christmas presents. Probably not Jamie. He'd probably murdered his mum and sold her off in pieces. We sat and wrapped crack, and the water splashed against the side of the boat, and the sun shone through the dirty windows and the bars made stripey shadows across the floor.

Angharad

On the bus, the rest of me started shaking. I wondered how my dad coped at work. I guessed you must just get used to being scared. Or knowing my dad, just not notice the scary people. Or assume that they were doing their best in difficult circumstances.

I got off the bus near the station. I went back in the Costa and ordered a cup of tea. The Costa felt safe and familiar now. I took the tea outside and sat in the sun feeling like a normal person.

I must have sat there, all alone, outside the Costa in Worcester, for at least fifteen minutes before I thought to look at my phone. I had two missed calls from Jake and a message telling me to call him back. I wasn't sure I could cope with a conversation just then but I didn't want him worrying so I texted to tell him I was okay, coming home, and I'd call later. My battery was at thirty two per cent.

I sat for ages, trying to remember everything the girl had said. When it had come to it, I had been nervous – terrified – about seeing Faith again, but not seeing her and not knowing what had happened to her was worse. I needed to find her. Or someone did. Maybe someone less scared. The girl hadn't really stopped me worrying, it felt more like there was a whole other world where girls had dreadlocks and men were something to be scared of and suddenly I was way out of my depth. This was more like I'd been imagining.

I wondered if Faith had just not been told about the terrible slippery slope of drugs or if she just assumed that those stories didn't apply to her. I was finding it harder and harder to have much patience with Marie, she seemed not to have bothered with quite a lot of what I thought was the stuff normal parents did. No wonder Faith didn't know which sort of dress to wear to church. I was starting to think that maybe Faith had never really been to church before, that she was no kind of Christian at all, and that Marie was a liar. I didn't know why you would pretend to be a church goer if you weren't. Our church is friendly and welcoming to everyone. There's no need to lie to try and fit in.

I thought at first that I was imagining it when I saw the girl from Broadway again. She was on the other side of the road, but she stopped dead to stare at me. Someone behind swore at her, but she didn't seem to notice and just carried on staring. I wasn't sure what to do. I waved at her, hoping she wouldn't come and start telling me about Phil again. I'm not a judgemental person but it can be hard not to be a bit judgemental with some people. She waved back, a bit awkwardly, then carried on. Every few steps she looked back over her shoulder. I was a bit freaked out too. I was getting really fed up of being scared. I was so tired. I finished my tea and went in to get another one. I sat inside this time, just in case the dreadlocks girl came back and I needed to hide so I didn't have to listen to her.

Faith

After we had a massive pile of wraps, Jamie took them out into the kitchen. I was trying to decide whether to nick some. I wouldn't usually, but it seemed rude not to, with it all sitting around like that. While he was gone, Brad looked over at me. 'So, girlie, what do you think? Are you in?'

And then his phone rang.

Angharad

I had a smoothie, because they're expensive and my mum would be furious at the waste of money and my dad would be sad because of the environmental impact or something. They always had good reasons why we were never allowed to do anything normal. Weirdly the smoothie felt like the most rebellious part of the day so far.

The smoothie wasn't as nice as I'd expected. I was annoyed, but I had to admit my mum was right. I added that to the list of things my mum was right about: smoothies, cities being scary. Things she had been wrong about: no-one had even noticed my slutty outfit, drugs turned out not to just be for baddies (although, in her defence, sometimes for baddies). The importance of mirrors. When I left home I was going to get a big one, so I could actually see what I looked like every single time I left the house. It wouldn't magically make me fashionable but it couldn't make things worse.

When I left the Costa, I realised that I was getting used to Worcester. I was coping with walking between all the people and not looking at their eyes and not saying anything as you passed them. At first it had felt rude, but I guess if you live in a city you can't say hello to everyone or you'd never get anywhere.

I saw the girl with the dog again, sitting in a doorway. I was surprised when she waved – maybe everyone in Worcester wasn't unfriendly. And then I noticed the muscly man in the white t-shirt behind me.

His t-shirt was so white that I accidentally glanced straight at him. Instead of looking away like everyone else, he stared back. I felt like I'd done something wrong. I turned and kept walking, fast.

When I looked back, he was still behind me, not too close, still glaring at me. I didn't know what to do. There was no reason to feel scared, but I did. I knew bad things happened in cities and I felt like one of them was about to happen to me. It was too much. I wasn't brave enough.

My knees felt shaky. I kept walking. I could see the station and I just had to walk up the hill and across the car park to it. Surely people couldn't just attack other people in cities? Or maybe they could, it's the kind of thing that happened on the news. I wanted to phone Jake but I didn't want to stop and get my phone out. I could feel my breath getting panicky.

And then I saw another man, on the other side of the car park, and he was staring at me too. When he saw me looking at him, he started laughing. I couldn't stop looking. He was waving at me, and it took me a minute to understand that the silver thing in his hand was a knife.

And I didn't want to panic but it was too late and I was running, as fast as I could, up to the station. As if the station was going to magically make me safe. And I couldn't look back or sideways in case I tripped, and my knees were shaking so much that I could hardly run and my chest was thumping and I could feel the panic inside me. I could hear the footsteps behind me, and he was laughing again, as if we were playing a game.

And I got to the station doors and they slid open and inside was Sam. 'Sam!' I threw myself towards him.

'Angharad,' he said in his nice, familiar Llanyfenni voice.

I put my face on his chest and he put his arms round me, awkwardly. He smelt of sweat and deodorant. As if he'd been in a small space with geeky boys. But I didn't want to let him go. After a minute he took his arms away. We stood together, silently, then he started walking away, towards the ticket barrier. I looked back. I didn't see the men.

'The train goes in seventeen minutes,' he said.

I followed him, too close, I didn't want to be on my own again. We stood awkwardly on the platform. I wanted to be as close to Sam as I could possibly be. I was still shaking. There were a lot of things I wanted to ask him. 'Sam…'

He looked carefully at the concrete. 'Yes?'

'Thank you.'

'I was getting a sandwich.' He looked back down the platform sadly. 'It fell out of my hand when you cwtched me.'

I felt terrible. I didn't know how to make it right. I had made Sam lose his sandwich, made him hug me, and now I was making him talk to me. I couldn't stop myself though. 'Why are you here?'

'Insomnia.'

He looked briefly at my face. 'Gaming thing. I'm in a team. Christian gamers.'

As if he needed to explain because he thought that I would be judgemental about a gaming competition. 'Were you here? In Worcester?'

He nodded. 'Only changing trains.'

I wished I could stop talking. I was even annoying myself. 'Your mum says you're really good.'

He nodded again. I sat still, so as not to bother him. I couldn't stop shaking.

Faith

I was pretty pissed off when Jamie and Brad just fucked off. Well, at first I was happy, when I assumed I could help myself to a bit of crack and some of Brad's dollar. But then it turned out they were going to lock the kitchen door with some massive padlock. Once they'd slammed shut the metal door out of the boat, and I heard them putting another padlock on that, I started to get a bit freaked out. But I've had worse, and whenever I'm feeling down I can always think about that Robert Dyas advert from 2015 with the gays. And the straights. And then I thought about Angharad's nipples in those unfashionable dresses and then a bit about how big the world is and how tiny we are when you think about it.

And when I'd finished that I went over to the window to see if I could wave at someone to rescue me, if I decided I wanted rescuing. But the glass was really thick and filthy dirty on the outside and the bars looked pretty sturdy and there wasn't much out there anyway. A factory on the other side of the canal. The houses, with no cars in the drives and no signs of life.

A boat went past, but they were too busy shouting at each other about something I couldn't hear to be paying any attention to whether a teenage girl was being kidnapped. If I was being kidnapped, I wasn't exactly sure. They were being very nice to me, if I was a prisoner, but also, I was still here and locked up. I sighed. Kidnapping seemed a bit of a dramatic word, for what had happened.

Brad had winked at me as he padlocked the kitchen, but he did still lock the door. I went to look at the door, just in case it would open, but that definitely wasn't happening. And then I wandered around the room a bit, in case they'd left anything interesting lying around which they obviously hadn't, being a pair of cunts. And then I saw something bright red on the floor. My heart went weird before my brain figured out what it was. And then my brain went pretty weird too, like it was trying to make connections that just didn't seem to be there.

Somehow, for some reason, one of Daria's big flowery, glittery, stickery hair clips was lying, all by itself, in a dirty corner of the room.

Angharad

The train to Hereford was nearly empty. I sat trying to work out what had happened. I couldn't see why two men would have been following me to the train station. But I also couldn't see why I would have imagined it. I don't normally imagine I'm being followed.

When I checked my phone, I'd had a reply from Jake. 'what time u get home?'

I replied and then my phone cut out. The battery had finally given up. Sam and I sat silently all the way to Hereford. I bought some sweets and we sat on the platform against a wall waiting for our train. It felt nice, a bit like being back at church. Peaceful. And safe. I leaned my head back and closed my eyes and didn't open them till I heard footsteps marching towards me.

Seeing Jake towering over me was so exciting that it took a minute to realise that he wasn't smiling. I introduced him to Sam and they shook hands, Sam looking awkward and Jake glaring at him. And we all stood there until we heard the train. Sam walked off without saying goodbye. I realised I was holding my breath and waiting for Jake to tell me what I had done wrong, but instead he waited until the doors had shut and then gave me one of his big hugs. It was lovely. He was rubbing my back as if I was a kid. I felt my muscles melting against him. 'I couldn't let you get the train back on your own,' he said. 'Come on.'

We walked out of the station and sat on a bench and I told him all about it. When I got to the bit about finding the house, he put his arm around me. 'That's when you phoned me?'

I leant into his side. I liked the way he smelt so much. 'Yeah.'

I told him about the woman and what she'd said about Faith going off with Brad. And Jed and Phil taking her phone. 'Wow!' he said. 'Spooky stuff, Angharad.'

But he said it like you would if you were watching it on TV. So I told him about the men by the station. I could feel him tense up next to me. He took his arm away and looked at me, looking very sincere. 'I should have been there,' he said.

'Well, then I saw Sam and it was okay.'

'Sam? That kid on the train?'

'Yeah.'

'What is he, some kind of superhero?'

'I was just pleased to see him.'

'Fucking hell!'

I was confused. Sam had helped me. 'Jake, are you jealous?'

'Why would I be jealous? Of a kid? I feel bad because I should have been there, and I wasn't, and then you needed me. I could have sorted it all out for you.'

I couldn't understand why he seemed to be angry with me about that. I tried to make it okay. 'Well, they probably weren't going to do much.'

'You made it sound like they were going to mug you.'

'Yeah. But they couldn't have really hurt me.'

'Not outside the station,' he agreed.

I tried not to remember how scared I'd been. 'But I was really glad to see Sam.'

'Yeah. So have you and him ever…?'

I wondered what he was thinking. 'Ever what?'

He shrugged. 'Well, ever, you know, gone out together? Slept together? Ever let him finger you?'

I felt like he'd slapped me. 'No.'

'Okay,' he nodded, then carried on as if it was nothing.

I wondered if that's what Jake thought about me, that I was the sort of girl who would just do that with anyone. Though, to be fair, it was possible that that was Jake's experience of girls. Sometimes I forgot not all girls were Christians. Jake was looking at me. 'Sorry, sweetheart.'

'I didn't do anything with Sam.'

He nodded. 'I'm sorry. I was just jealous. Thinking about you and that pillock.'

I thought about defending Sam, but I didn't want Jake to get cross with me again. And I was a bit in love with the idea of him being jealous. Jealous of Sam, for being with me. 'It doesn't matter,' I said.

I smiled at him. He smiled back, 'So we know that Faith is with this Jamie?'

He put his arm along the back of the bench, behind me. I could feel his bare arm across my back. I looked down at our legs, pressed up against each other. I realised I had my hands in my lap, as if I was praying. Jake carried on talking. I guessed he was probably less distracted by how close we were sitting. 'Maybe the Journey's End is a pub. It's the kind of thing they call a Spoons.'

'Spoons?'

Jake rolled his eyes. 'Wetherspoons. It's like you're from the Victorians or something.'

Wetherspoons, Costa, Starbucks (in town, not just on the bypass). H&M. All things we seemed to be missing, that would have made us a proper town. And the things we had, that I thought proper towns probably didn't. A market, for sheep and cows, in the middle of town. A shop that sold mainly lambing buckets – whatever they are – and sacks of carrots, potatoes and coal. Though now I'd seen Worcester properly, I felt that our town had its benefits. No one had even threatened me a tiny bit there.

I had never seen anyone with a knife, or even heard anyone talk about one. Apart from the summer the home educators discovered whittling and everyone had to have a pocket knife. The knives were supposed to be for whittling, but mainly they were for comparing, and waving around casually. Obviously I didn't have one, because we weren't interested in fashion (Mum) and we preferred not to carry weapons (Mum and Dad, unusually united in their reasons). Dad did buy me an Action Man, in case I wanted to express myself in a more active way, but he had taken away the toy gun, and sewn a nice t-shirt for him. All the pocket knives disappeared in the weeks after a four year old sliced the end of his finger off and no one ever mentioned them again.

Jake also seemed to be thinking, presumably about something more interesting than Action Men. 'You must have freaked that girlie right out.'

I thought Jake should remember whose side he was on. 'She freaked me out!'

He smiled at me again, and rubbed his hand on my shoulder. 'I know, babe. You were very brave.'

He pulled out his tobacco and started rolling a cigarette. He looked over at me. 'Do you mind if I smoke here? I can move if it bothers you.'

'It's fine.'

So he sat next to me and I didn't cough until a tiny bit when he'd nearly finished.

'If you're worried about Faith, we need to go back to Worcester, I guess,' he said.

'We', I noticed, happily. Though the 'need to go back to Worcester' bit wasn't quite so cheering.

'I might talk to my dad,' I said, testing out the idea.

I'd been thinking on the train and it seemed the sensible thing to do. If Faith didn't have her phone, and had been staying with some guy whose girlfriend was terrified of him, and possibly hunted down girls in the street then it felt fairly obvious to me that the police might be the best people to deal with the situation. And Faith might need help quickly. From the look on Jake's face, you'd think I'd said I might eat a slug. 'Jeez, Angh! Don't be twp.'

'But my dad will know how to find her.'

He shook his head. 'The police won't be interested. They'll think Faith's some kind of criminal if you tell them about the drugs, and then they definitely won't help.'

I wasn't sure my dad really counted as some anonymous 'they' – he's my dad – but I guessed Jake might be right. Recently I'd heard Dad muttering about drug gangs and teenagers and the muttering didn't exactly sound approving. It was hard for me to imagine him thinking Faith selling cannabis was a wholesome teen activity. And even if he was understanding, I wasn't sure the rest of Llanyfenni's police force would be. I stayed quiet.

Jake was looking at me as if I was a child again. 'Angharad,' he said, as if he was being very patient. 'I know your dad's a copper.'

I nodded helpfully. Jake was running his fingers up and down my arm, which was a bit distracting, but I tried to concentrate on what he was saying. 'And your Dad's a good bloke, I know that.'

I felt like my whole body was tingling. Jake kept talking. 'But you don't understand how it is. The police won't give a shit about Faith. They'll do nothing, like when Wynn's digger was nicked, or they'll go off at the deep end and just arrest everyone. The police don't give a shit about people like Faith.'

I was sure that wasn't true. 'The police are just making sure people obey the law, Jake. They're the good guys.'

Jake turned sideways to look at me properly. 'Angharad, stop thinking about your dad. Think about the guys he works with. Think about Dan Davies, and that Matt. Why do you think they wanted to be in the police? Do you think they want to help people? Help old women across the road? What does Dan Davies think about Faith?'

I thought about Dan Davies, sitting in our kitchen, drinking lager he'd confiscated from someone in the park and the way he talked about the people he arrested. Thought about him laughing about when he got trained to use the riot gear down in Cwmbran. Thought about him looking at me, up and down, as if he could see under my clothes. But that didn't mean that every policeman was like that. I knew Jake was wrong, but I didn't say anything.

He carried on grumpily, 'And then you'll tell him about me, and then he'll think I'm just some dodgy bloke and then he'll never want you to have anything to do with me.'

I thought that was probably true as well. I couldn't imagine my dad thinking Jake was a good thing at all. 'So let's just figure out where Faith is and check she's okay?' He tipped his head on the side. 'You and me?'

'Okay.'

'Okay,' he smiled at me. 'Oh, and I finished things with Ella, I know it was stressing you out, me and her,' he said.

I wondered if he was really as casual as he sounded. And would he really split up with someone because I didn't like it? But if he had, then he must really care about what I thought. 'Oh, right.' I hoped my tone didn't sound as flattered as I felt. 'Are you okay?'

He laughed and stood up, then reached down and patted me on the head. 'Right. We should get going? I've borrowed a mate's car for a couple of days. You should phone your parents and tell them something.'

Faith

When Brad and Jamie got back, they weren't saying much but they marched in like dogs that have won a fight, all cocky. 'Still here?' Jamie asked, sarkily. 'No knight in shining armour for you?'

I ignored him, and smiled at Brad. He rolled his eyes at Jamie. 'Sorry we had to leave you, we thought there was an issue. But there was no issue. Just Daria, being a big fucking drama queen. Well, only a small issue and it's gone now. Dealt with.'

'I didn't know you knew Daria,' I said, still thinking about the hair clip, still holding it in my hand. Brad looked at it and I guess that was where everything went a bit tits up. Jamie rolled his eyes. 'Well, aren't you the little detective,' he said and disappeared back out the door.

Brad sighed and sat down. 'It's complicated, Faith. But I'll explain.'

I heard Jamie thudding about on the roof. Brad was looking away from me. 'The thing is, Daria has some problems.'

Like that was fucking news to me. Brad was still looking sad, but I was pretty sure that he wasn't, actually, sad. I was pretty sure that he actually didn't give a shit. 'Daria came to us, for help.'

It was hard to imagine, little Daria thinking Brad and Jamie were going to help her. But also easy, if I thought about how Daria always seemed to see the best in people, and never seemed to notice what was actually going on right under her nose. 'Pharmaceutical help,' Brad said, and grinned at me. 'Which obviously, Jamie and I are ideally placed to provide.'

'Ah.' I felt bad, thinking about that. I imagined poor Daria, coming to Jamie, behind Phil's back. Looking for help to get through the day. Help not to break, when things were too hard. I wished I'd paid her more attention.

And then, suddenly, the whole room started shaking and an engine started. I tried not to jump, looked across at Brad, who was grinning again. 'There's no need to worry, Faith. We're just moving the boat a bit. Somewhere a bit quieter.'

The boat lurched forwards. Brad was watching out the window and I watched the factory move away. He passed me a beer and grabbed two more. 'There's always problems, Faith,' he said, 'but we have to make them into opportunities.'

I thought maybe he was joking, but he sounded exactly like one of Jed's lectures. 'Still, onwards and upwards, isn't it? We'll just get you somewhere safe and out of the way. Then we can have a chat about how to move forwards.'

He sounded a bit absent though – a businessman who was actually trying to slope off to watch some porn. 'You can stay in here. Just relax and enjoy the ride,' he said in the same way, then disappeared out the door. I heard him lock it behind him.

I lay on the floor and watched the sky pass by. There was too much to think about. Everything felt strange, like nothing was real any more. I was pretty sure that I had accidentally, definitely, got kidnapped.

I woke up when we crashed gently into something. Brad came bouncing back in, looking cheerier. 'Have we parked?' I asked.

I was feeling pretty woozy. Vodka and beer and spliffs are all awesome, but I really wanted a big glass of water. Jamie marched in right behind Brad. 'Moored, Faith. It's a boat not a fucking car.'

They were both hyped up, Brad's mouth was twitching. Great. 'Come on, then,' he said, 'Get up, get up, let's get moving.'

I rubbed my eyes and got up, put my coat on. It felt like a bit of a buffer between me and the world. It felt like I was going to need it.

We got outside and Jamie offered me a ciggie and we all lit up. We were in some kind of flash redevelopment. Those modern flats, with shiny silver balconies and tables and chairs and plants with fairy lights wrapped round them. No one was around. You could smell the canal. That stale water smell always makes me think of death but that's probably just me.

I didn't say anything, just stood there, watching the smoke and breathing in and out, hoping it wasn't all as bad as it was starting to seem. Brad was standing next to me, twitching his leg. 'Like it?'

Obviously I didn't like it. Who actually likes places like that? But I must have been a bit edgy because I nodded. Brad grinned at me. 'Top floor flat. We struck pretty lucky. You're going to love this, Faith.'

I pushed down the scared feeling in my stomach. 'Are we going to a party up there, then?' I asked.

They both looked at me, like they were trying to figure out what was wrong with me. I raised my eyebrows at them. Brad laughed. 'Yeah, we're going to a party.'

And he winked at me, and I chucked my cigarette down on the pavement and rubbed my foot on it. 'Come on then, lads.'

We went up in some fancy swanky lift, all shiny silver and mirrors. I looked like shit. My hair needed washing and my eyebrows were a state. Waterproof mascara was smeared all round my eyes. I stared into my eyes. Brave and strong, don't think about it, I told myself. Nothing can touch you, don't let them get to you.

We stopped at the top floor. The lift door opened and we were in a corridor. It smelt of new carpet. There were a few doors then the corridor turned a corner. It was weirdly quiet. Like a graveyard. Brad had a key for the last door. We went in. I let Brad go first, seemed sensible. It was silent inside and nearly dark. There was a big kitchen living room thing, like something out of a magazine. Some bloke was asleep on the settee, I could hear him breathing, loudly. There was a wet stain at the top of his legs. I was sure it couldn't be a good sign that I was back in a world where I could smell piss.

'No party?' I asked Brad.

He shrugged. 'Nah, not really. But it's an awesome flat, isn't it?'

He turned the light on and we both looked at the man. He

was old, maybe fifty, and his face was red and his socks were dirty. There was a crack pipe near him on the floor and Brad shrugged. 'Don't worry about him. He just lives here.'

I looked at Brad. I had no idea what was going on now, but I wasn't going to ask in case I found out. He was looking round at the flat. 'So nice,' he said. 'It's good to have somewhere to bring people to impress them, you know what I mean?'

I looked at the sleeping man, at the dirty work surfaces, down at the floor, which was covered in stuff that had been spilt and not cleaned up. 'Yeah,' I said. 'So nice.'

Jamie took my arm, too hard, and pulled me to a door. 'This is yours. For now.'

He pushed me in, and turned the light on but didn't follow me. He shut the door. There was a bed, a double, with all matching bedding on it. A wardrobe, and a chest of drawers. It was all pretty surreal.

I took the pillow and jammed it under the door as much as I could. It wouldn't stop anyone getting in but it might make enough noise to wake me up. The sun was still high but I was suddenly too tired to think about much else. I didn't want to lie on the bed, it looked dirty too. The floor didn't look any better but I lay down on it with my head on my bag. I didn't fancy taking my shoes and coat off or turning off the light. Even with my coat on every part of me felt cold and I couldn't stop shaking.

I was even colder when I woke up. And stiff. Didn't know what time it was because no phone. I really hated Jamie and Brad right now. It was still light though. I looked out the window. It was dirty but the view was pretty cool. I wondered what Jamie and Brad actually did, to make everything so dirty. Remembered Jed's lovely clean floors. I wanted coffee and a smoke and a piss.

Turned out there was a tiny bathroom, an en suite. Which would have been more exciting if it wasn't totally disgusting. Broken lipstick lying on the side of the sink. I washed my face *too, trying not to touch the sink. Lit a ciggie and smoked it sitting on the floor. Still didn't fancy the bed much. It gave me the creeps, not sure why. I sat and listed things in my head that had happened to me that had been worse than last night, that I'd survived. It didn't make me feel as good as I'd hoped. When you put all the shit things in your life together in a list, it can just make you realise that there's been a lot of shit things.*

I wasn't sure whether going out of the room was a good idea but I didn't fancy hanging around in there either. And I really wanted a fucking coffee. And I was so sick of hanging round waiting for bad stuff to happen, maybe I needed to take a bit of positive action. Be the change I wanted to see.

I listened at the door before I tried to open it. I couldn't hear anything. I felt sick at the thought of going out, but being locked in was worse. I pushed the handle down very slowly. I realised I was praying for the door to open. Maybe not to Angharad's god, but definitely to someone. It opened.

There was no one in the corridor and no one in the big room. The noisy breathing man was gone. There was a big window and a balcony outside but it was locked. The front door was locked too, unless I just couldn't figure out how to open it. Sometimes fancy doors are a bit weird, but I tried every way to get it open that I could think of. Even now, with the sunshine creeping in, nothing in this flat felt normal. Found a clock on the oven. It said 05.36. It might have been right.

I turned the kettle on. There was a fancy coffee machine but I had no idea how that worked. The people I normally hang out with don't seem to own fancy coffee machines. The worktops were covered in spilt food and there was a dirty frying pan on the hob. I gave the mug a decent wash. I'd have bleached it if I could've found any bleach. I'm not some kind of clean freak but fuck knows who'd been drinking out of it. No milk.

I sat and drank it on the floor by the window. As if being on the floor meant I was safe. Had another cigarette. To be honest, I was still feeling sick, and I was fucking freaked out. No idea what was going on, and why they wanted me here.

I checked out the other rooms, carefully, tiptoeing along the hallway. Two other bedrooms, no one in either. Stuff in both though. Women's stuff. Make up and clothes. Not much though. Nothing nice. A vibrator on one of the beds. Jeez. I hoped that it was cleaner than the rest of the flat, but it didn't look it. I didn't go poking around in the cupboards. I got the drift. This place wasn't a spa and probably didn't belong to some nice rich widow who was going to want to adopt me. Though I had no idea what it actually was. Some shitty brothel? Did they really think I was going to be up for that? I sat back down by the window and smoked the rest of my cigs and then lay by the window in the sunlight and waited for something to happen. Down on the canal the boats were shuttling along and someone was running. I hoped they were keeping an eye open for the dog shit.

Bit fucking weird, having a flat like this and then not even using it. I made myself another coffee, and hunted about to see if anyone had left any ciggies anywhere. I didn't look in the bedside drawers, which was kind of the obvious place. It was also the obvious place to store all your kinky shit, and I wasn't sure I fancied seeing that, however much I wanted a smoke.

Angharad

Jake had wandered away to get more tobacco and a parking ticket. He had laughed when I asked if I could borrow his phone and then handed it over. 'If you go prying, you've only yourself to blame if you find stuff you don't like.'

I walked down the side of the building and then sat on the ground, in the shade, thinking about what Jake had said. Thought about Jake being jealous, at being angry with Sam for looking after me. About Jake wanting to look after me in Worcester himself.

I watched the cars going past and someone in a massive four-by-four trying to park in a space where it didn't fit. Some things were obviously the same everywhere.

I thought about the beginning of May, when I had woken up on my fifteenth birthday and mum had said we could go to the cinema as a treat. I had sat there drinking lemonade and eating a smuggled in packet of popcorn in an old theatre with a big screen installed and wondered if my life was ever going to start. And now it had, and it was a lot lonelier than I'd imagined. Outside the church, things did turn out to be darker and scarier and more complicated.

I thought about Faith, smiling and biting on a burger as if she was a happy, friendly tiger and about how she looked, running away down the hill, her dress blowing up past her knees and her not caring at all. Probably not even noticing.

I thought about the girl in Worcester, all tiny and fragile but talking like she was responsible for fixing the world. I thought about Sam, and how gentle and quiet he was. And then back to Jake's face, all tight and tense, when he thought about Sam touching me. And in the whole of the day, that was the bit that kept going round and round in my head, his eyes on mine, as if he was confessing something important, showing me that he cared about me.

I put in my home number carefully, to prove to myself

that Jake was wrong to think I would go prying. My mum's voice was muffled and I could hear her chopping something. 'Are you having a nice time?' she asked brightly.

I remembered just in time not to tell her the truth. I still hadn't found out how old Jake was but he was old enough to freak them out. I thought for a few minutes about whether maybe he was old enough to count as a responsible adult but even my optimistic dad might have some awkward questions about that. Took a breath and lied, trying to be just as bright as her. Then I ended the call and closed my eyes. I didn't want to think about my mum, and being at home.

Instead, I made myself think about Jake's fingers on my arm, and Jake's face when he told me he was jealous, and Jake and I in Worcester. I imagined my mum's face if I told her that I was with Jake Morgan, and all the home ed girls' faces if they saw us driving past. I imagined casually saying to someone, 'Yeah, well, I was with Jake.' I thought about being the one running across a sunny field towards him in front of a crowd of people.

I wished that I had had a chance to properly plan which underwear I could wear, to make me look better, and what I could say, to make me sound better. I wished I had time to practise how to be someone better and cooler and sexier. Someone more like Ella.

I wished that I was less scared about what might happen in Worcester when we were alone.

Jamie

So if we have a leak in our little ship, it's Faith. Am sick of dealing with that little bitch.

Faith

The sun was behind the flat and the window was finally in shadow. I looked for food and found some pot noodles. It could have been worse. I wasn't going to check the date on them but the lid was still stuck on so I hoped for the best. I found some rubber gloves, still in a packet, so I started cleaning. I'm sick of cleaning up after other people, but it was better than thinking. And I only did the kitchen, I stayed well out of the disturbing bedrooms. When it was a bit cleaner I stopped and looked at my reflection in the window. Yellow marigolds, white summer dress and hair all over the place. I was a mess. I leant my head against the window, which smelt nice and vinegary now. I wasn't going to cry, because there's no fucking point. There's never any fucking point.

I woke up when Brad came back. He laughed when he saw me. 'Aw, my sleeping beauty! Sorry about all this, we've had to sort a few things out.'

I sat up and watched him. He seemed very cheerful. 'I brought you an ice cream.'

He handed me a Magnum. White chocolate. I wanted to say no, but I wanted the Magnum more. He went over to the fridge and put some milk in it. 'Do you feel okay? Better after a sleep?' he asked, sounding like he actually ca red.

I wondered, when was the last time anyone had asked me that? Pretty sure no one ever had. Wondered when someone had last bought me an ice cream, just because they were at the shop, thinking about me. Wondered if I was just going to be a useless pile of self-pity now. Brad was whistling as he put the kettle on. His t-shirt was still shiny white. He must have more than one. He was wearing shorts that showed off his thick white thighs. His sunglasses were pushed up onto the top of his head.

'Coffee, princess?'

I nodded and held out my mug for him. Finished the Magnum. Felt a bit sick. He was chatting away. 'So, earlier was a bit messy, Jamie and me overreacted to something. It's not easy, Faith, trying to keep stuff together here and then setting up a new business too.'

I wondered if he'd brought any more food. He looked down at me, as if he could read my mind. 'Sausages?'

I nodded. He brought the coffee over and passed it down. I realised he was looking down my dress, at my tits. I let him, there didn't seem to be any harm in it. He was pottering away in the kitchen while he talked. 'It's a tricky time for us. Lots of dollar ahead, once things are set up, so it's worth the work, but we need everything all neat. All ready to move forward.'

He came over to the window and sat down by me, too close. 'I'm not saying it's your fault –' he sounded like he thought I needed reassuring – 'but you've screwed things up a bit. We're disappointed in you.'

I was disappointed in myself, really. I'm usually pretty good at knowing what's going on, but I was well confused. Fancy flats, boats, buckets of cash, it felt a long way from Phil's lounge. 'Why?'

Brad's shorts were tight against all those muscles. He grinned at me, as if he was telling me a joke. 'I guess your referee was a bit out of date. And now you've been a naughty girl, Faith.'

Brad put his hand on my thigh, squeezed it thoughtfully. His hand was hot, and huge. I couldn't breathe. 'Not to worry though, we'll get it all sorted.'

His voice was hoarse, like he had a cold coming on. Or like he was enjoying sitting there, with his big, hot hand on my leg. My throat was dry. I didn't understand what was going on. What had happened to nice, chatty Brad? Who was going to give me some dollar and send me back to Llanyfenni, with money for the electric meter?

He took his hand off my leg to roll a joint and passed it over. I felt like I was balancing over deep water. I wasn't keen on having anything of his in my mouth, in case it gave him ideas, but I took the joint anyway. 'What have I supposed to have done?'

He grinned at me, not unsympathetically. 'Not so cocky now?'

I shrugged and he winked at me. 'You're just too gobby, I think. I like it. I like you. But we can't just have randoms rocking up all over the place asking questions. It's not cool, telling everyone your business, having some girl hunting you all over Worcester.'

For a moment I felt pleased, to have someone hunting for me all over Worcester, that maybe I was going to get rescued, like a princess in a tower. Finally my Disney princess moment. He laughed loudly. His laugh was really starting to get on my tits. 'I felt bad about your phone, Faith, I really did, but I see now it was for the best. We're learning as we go. You can probably tell.'

'Who's looking for me?'

He looked at me, mouth twisted. 'You're a smart cookie, Faith. Don't screw this up more than you have. What you need to do now is just lie low a bit. Lie low with me and Jamie and let the dust blow over. It's lucky we've got this place. Keep you nice and safe, here, with us.'

Nice and safe with Brad and Jamie. Sounded like a kids' TV show.

'You like it here? It cost that bloke some real fucking dollar. Guess he won't be buying another one now!'

He was chortling away. I nodded. Drank the coffee. 'So what's going on, then?' I asked.

He looked at me, at my face, and then lower down. I looked back at him. I was tired and my make up was shit and I'd slept in my dress, but at least I'd taken the Marigolds off. I was still pretty sure he wasn't going to have seen anything better, but I wasn't so sure any more that that was a good thing. His eyes met mine. 'I'll be honest with you, Faith. Probably nothing great for a bit. We've got to make sure everything's cool. All the loose ends tied up.'

He winked and then turned away from me and sat back, against the window. 'But you'll be alright, you'll be grateful you stuck with us.'

I thought about saying something cocky to show him he was wrong, but I didn't. Maybe that meant I was learning already. 'Can't I go home?'

My voice sounded pathetic. Brad didn't look unsympathetic, to be fair to him. But he wasn't exactly offering to drive me back to Llanyfenni or anything. He shook his head. 'No. You just need to learn whose side you're on. Like a family, Faith. You might not always like it, but we're in it together. We need to know we can trust you. Blabbing to interfering do-gooder Welsh girls isn't helping you.'

It took me a minute to realise that interfering do-gooder Welsh girls had to be Angharad. It had to be. There was no one else I knew even a bit that anyone would ever describe as a do-gooder. Unbelievable. Angharad, in Worcester. Looking for me. That was very brave of her.

I realised Brad was still talking. 'Be on my side. Stop fighting it and you'll be laughing like the rest of us. Just a tip. You don't owe Phil and Jed anything. They're not your friends. They're snowflake rich kids. Different world. It's not like mummy and daddy are going to look after you and me, we're on our own. It'll be okay.'

He patted my leg again, laughing to himself as if he had said something funny. I felt like I was supposed to thank him. I wondered what it would take to stop me wanting to go home, to stop me even thinking about Llanyfenni. What they could do to me. And how they'd know when they'd finished and they'd let me out of here. And what would happen then. And I couldn't help wondering what it would be like to have a mum who might have noticed you'd gone, and not just because there was no one putting money on the gas. A mum who'd have phoned the police, be looking for you.

Not like my poor mum, who was probably sitting in the dark or paddling through a puddle of some man's piss trying to get to the sink.

But then I thought of Angharad, in some nerdy outfit, looking at everything and not saying much and quietly figuring stuff out. Looking for me.

Brad sighed. 'Make it easy on yourself. Lose the attitude. Don't ask questions. And stop blabbing to those people. You're moving on, Faith. On and up.'

It wasn't like she'd find me, she'd probably already given up, but it sounded like she might have tried, and that was sweet.

'Just do as you're told, and when you get out of here keep doing it. It's not rocket science. You're good. You know it. It's all going to be good. Better than good. It's going to be fucking awesome.'

We finished the joint. He turned to face me and slowly moved his big meaty hand on my leg again. I moved my leg. He shrugged and put it back.

'We can be a good team,' he said, still squeezing. Dick.

I don't know why I was so freaked out. It's not like this is something new. Men have been putting their sweaty hands on my legs since I hit puberty. It's not a big deal. I can handle it.

He was leaning back against the window. 'You and me, Faith. Making a shitload of money. We can do what we want then. Go on some all you can eat holiday in Spain. Go to some fancy restaurant in London. Buy nice stuff for this place, stuff that you like. You could have a room here, if you wanted.'

I wondered why he was so sure that I was the person that he wanted to do all this stuff with. Like he had before, he seemed to know what I was thinking. 'You're just a kid, I know that, Faith. I won't try anything. But I'm not that much older than you, really. And we're two of a kind. I was a feisty little cunt when I was fifteen. I know what it's like. Phil says you pretty much look after your mum, that's the kind of girl I want. Someone who does what needs to be done. Looks after family.'

I've been come on to by a lot of blokes in a lot of different ways. But this was the weirdest. I wasn't even sure if he actually wanted to fuck me at all, or if he just wanted someone on his side. Someone to talk to, and plan with and to cook for and sit with. I sighed.

He got up, cracked eggs into a pan. I watched him, imagining us in Spain, by a pool, drinking cocktails. Imagining being with someone who would probably kill anyone who hurt me. He was looking across at me. 'Not like a couple. Not yet. You don't need to freak out. It's just—' he shrugged. 'Just all these fucking dollars and no one to share it with.'

And he brought me over a plateful of food, and I sat cross legged on the floor and ate it fast, before it could get taken away. He sat beside me, watching me. And then I put the plate down, and shut my eyes and let him get on with touching my leg and tried to think what I was going to do. There didn't seem any point thinking why I was here, and how I had screwed up to end up here. I needed to get out before I gave up wanting to.

Marie

A nice surprise today. One of Faith's friends phoned. He said someone might come and stay with me. A girl called Olly. I forgot to ask how long for. He said they could just sleep on the couch, and they'd give me a bit of money for my trouble. He said Faith was having a nice time. I wish she'd call.

Faith

I washed up. Brad leaned against the kitchen counter and looked approving. I wondered if what he actually wanted was a mum. Then we sat and played draughts. Brad couldn't believe I'd never played before. 'Not even when you were a kid?'

'Who taught you to play?' I asked.

'My uncle.'

'A proper uncle or an uncle that's fucking your mum?'

'Yeah, that kind.'

'Well, it's a dick move to laugh at people for not knowing how to do things.'

But I was laughing and so was he. 'There's loads of stuff I bet you don't know. Ever put a tampon in?'

Brad's mouth was hanging open, like he'd never heard the word before. 'Faith!' he said, shocked.

I grinned at him. I was glad when the door buzzer went because it was starting to feel like Brad and I may as well be married already. Brad looked at me. 'Are we cool?'

I nodded. 'Who is it?'

'You'll see. I'll introduce you.'

It was a kid. She looked about thirteen, shifty and spotty and white, carrying a rucksack. Brad grinned at her. 'Come in, meet Faith. She's been a naughty girl, but she's good now.'

The girl's eyes flicked up then away again. I didn't know if she wasn't interested, or just scared. 'Faith, this is Olly.' Brad winked. 'She's not really Olly. But let's pretend.'

Brad took Olly over to the corner and they whispered furiously at each other for a bit. Then she handed Brad some cash, and Brad reached under the sink and pulled out a box. He unlocked it and handed a bag over to the girl. 'You wanna play?' Brad asked, nodding over at me, and the draughts.

Olly shook her head. 'Not this time, mate,' Brad agreed. 'We'll have a proper catch up soon, though? When you get back? Get some pop in? Play some games.'

Olly nodded and skulked off out the door. Brad locked the door behind her. 'What sort of games?' I asked, sarcastically. 'Monopoly?'

Brad shrugged. 'Sometimes. Or I get the X-box out. She don't have much fun, it's nice for her. Like a youth club, sort of thing. She's going to earn me a shitload of dollar, it's the least I can do for the little sod.'

I tried not to wonder if I'd been like that kid when I was thirteen. I was pretty sure I hadn't. 'How many of them have you got?'

Brad shrugged. 'That's confidential information, Faith.'

But then he laughed. 'I'll be straight with you, babe, not many. Early days. Set the board up again.'

Jamie slid into the flat. I was beyond even being surprised that he was followed by Daria. Daria looked even more out of it than normal, and her pupils were huge. She stood inside the doorway, swaying. When she saw me, she screamed happily, and tried to run over. She was sort of staggering, like she'd had too much of something, and she got slower and slower. We all waited, while she lurched on. When I got bored waiting, I got up and walked to meet her. She hugged me. She smelt of weed and sweat and something else. It was hard to see that her being here was a good thing, but at least it might distract Brad from our beautiful future together.

I put her on the settee and went to put the kettle on. Brad was still sitting on the floor by the draughts board. 'Tea or coffee?' I asked him.

He stood up and came over, took the milk out. 'Go and sit with her. She's probably got stuff to tell you.'

We both looked at Daria. She was asleep. Brad shrugged and put teabags in three mugs. Jamie got a bottle of lager out the fridge. 'She's had a bit much,' he said. 'Got a bit carried away.'

Brad put a lot of sugar in a cup of tea and put it by Daria's feet. 'She'll be alright,' he told me. 'She gets like this.'

I couldn't understand why Daria would think getting like

that, around a scumbag like Jamie, was a good idea. I stayed stood up, by Brad. I didn't want them thinking that I was like Daria. 'You're not like her,' Brad said.

I hated the way he did that. I hated the way I wanted to stay near him, because it felt safer than being on my own. 'I'm nothing like her,' I agreed.

I gave her foot a bit of a kick, to make it clear. 'So she's finished with Phil now? Or is he going to turn up here too?'

Jamie shrugged. 'I figured it was best if she was with us for now.'

'With you and Brad? Or just with you?'

Jamie was looking pissed off again. 'No, Faith,' he said snarkily. 'I wouldn't touch that.'

Brad gave me a tiny wink. 'She's going to work for us. Take some stuff up country. Earn some dollar.'

'Is that what you want me to do?'

Brad laughed. 'You'd be wasted. Maybe at first, to get an idea of it, but we think you've got potential.'

Jamie rolled his eyes, took his coffee, downed it to show how hard he was and walked out the front door, slamming it behind him. Brad winked at me again. 'Guess I'll see you later,' he said. 'Take care of Daria, she'll be mardy when she comes round.'

'Leave the door unlocked?' I suggested, and he laughed.

I heard him lock it and then turn it to check. I had a swig of coffee and then sat down and waited for Daria to wake up.

Angharad

I wasn't sure Jake's mate's car would get all the way to Worcester. I didn't know much about cars but it seemed like some of the gears didn't really seem to be there all the time. Every now and then there would be a horrible noise and Jake would swear cheerfully. Jake drove too fast and didn't concentrate enough. When I asked if the car was going to be alright, he glowered at me. 'I'm a mechanic. I don't think you really need to worry about whether I can fix a car.'

That wasn't what I had meant, but I didn't ask again. Instead, I spent most of the drive worrying my heart would just stop before we got there. I wasn't sure Jake's first aid skills would be up to much. We had to listen to the music so loudly that my ears hurt. Sometimes he'd turn his head and grin at me and I'd pretend I hadn't noticed so he'd look back at the road quicker. About halfway there, he turned the music down and looked at me intently for a second. 'So, Angharad –'

I held my breath. He glanced forward for a second and then looked back at me when he asked, 'Do you just like girls? Or, you know, men too?'

I hadn't been expecting that. I realised I was gripping my leg tightly and tried to let go. I tried to think what I should say. I pressed myself back into the chair and tried to sound relaxed. 'Um.'

That wasn't a good start. Jake looked across and nodded encouragingly. 'Um,' I started again.

Jake looked pityingly at me. 'Never mind,' he said and patted my knee.

I sank into my humiliation, and then realised his hand was still on my knee. I said nothing and after a while he moved it back to the gear stick. 'You might feel different once you've kissed a man.'

I didn't look at him, but I could sense he was smiling.

Faith

Daria seemed delighted when she woke up and saw me. I was glad to see her too, which was weird because she wasn't exactly going to be any use to me. She was more worried about Phil than about telling me anything useful about what was going on and why she was here. 'I love him,' she said, 'I still really love him. Even after everything he's done to me.'

I didn't want to get her started on her list of the things she thought that Phil had done. I knew there was no point even trying to tell her that Phil was a slimy failure. That's not me being mean, that's just a true fact. She was staring into my eyes. 'He's not a bad man, I know he's not.'

I wondered what Phil would actually have to do before Daria would notice that Phil didn't give a shit about her. 'So what's happening with Jamie?'

She looked worried. 'He has a very confusing aura. I know he seems nice, but I've got a sense about these sorts of things. He's been very kind to me though.' She blushed. 'Sorry to tell you, Faith, but I think maybe he fancies me.'

I remembered then why I found Daria so massively annoying. She was shaking her head sadly. 'I'm sorry that you've had to find out like this.'

I wasn't sure if I was supposed to be jealous of her or Jamie. 'I don't fancy Jamie,' I said, just to be clear. 'Or you.'

She smiled at me and gave a quick little shrug, like we both knew I was pretending, but she was happy to go along with it. 'So what happened?' I asked.

'I should never have lied to Phil. He said no pills, but they're just so nice, and Jamie was really lush to me, gave me a special deal and everything. And Phil was so angry with me.'

I hadn't ever really noticed Phil getting angry about anything, ever. 'Are you sure he was angry?'

She nodded frantically. 'Yes! He said I was an ignorant, useless bitch.'

I still wasn't convinced. Phil said stuff like that to me all the time. She was peering at me carefully. 'After I told him about that Welsh girl.'

It took me a second to understand. 'Angharad?'

She nodded. 'Is that her name? Big Welsh girl, pretended she was coming to see Phil. Faith, is she your girlfriend? Because she's quite aggressive.'

I sighed. Maybe Daria didn't always see the best in people, after all. Or maybe only men. 'How did she look?'

'Sneaky.'

'Sneaky?'

'I didn't notice at first,' Daria looked doubtful. 'But she tricked me. And when I think about it, she had sneaky eyes.'

'Right. Apart from that?'

I wondered what I wanted to hear. That Angharad looked like she'd enjoyed kissing me so much that she'd come to Worcester to do it some more? I couldn't see why else she'd be here. I tried again to get some useful information from Daria. 'I really like her.'

Daria's mouth flopped open. 'That Welsh girl?'

I nodded. I waited. Daria shut her mouth and pursed her lips. 'Her jeans were weird.'

I smiled before I could stop myself. 'I know. Was she wearing those shoes?'

'Like big sandals? Jesus sandals?'

I nodded again. Daria was still looking like I'd hit her with a cod. 'You fancy that girl?'

'Yes.'

'But you kissed me?' Her eyebrows wrinkled together, like she was doing sums. 'And then you knew it could never happen between us, and now you fancy her?'

I didn't argue. Thinking about Angharad seemed to have made me patient. 'So, Daria, do you think she was looking for me because she liked me too?'

I knew this was the kind of thing that Daria could spend hours chatting about, even if no one else joined in at all. This time, I was happy to listen, while Daria talked about every bit of Angharad's aura – pink with a bit of black for her sneakiness – and her tone of voice and the way her eyes had moved when she said my name. Then we had another coffee and talked about why I liked her and what had happened between us and what happened after. 'And then you never saw her again?' Daria's mouth was open again. 'Like a fairy tale?'

We both thought about that. I didn't really know any fairy tales, so I was happy to listen to Daria on that one. In the end, she shook her head. 'Not really, I don't think. But very romantic.'

I was pleased that she'd been won over. I hadn't mentioned the church. Even though Daria believed in 5G causing cancer and that thinking bad thoughts made you ill, I was pretty sure her beliefs didn't include god. I wasn't sure mine did either really, seeing the way some of the women looked at me and my mum.

I was getting hungry again. 'What do Brad and Jamie actually do all day? Like, where are they?'

'They have a flat over in town. Imagine having two flats.'

'And the boat.'

'They're so cool,' Daria agreed.

I wanted to think that she was clueless but I couldn't forget how impressed I'd been with the boat. And I'd probably be more impressed with the flat if I wasn't pretty sure that it belonged to the pissy man. Maybe in exchange for the little tinfoil parcels.

'We're locked in,' I reminded both of us.

'I know! They said I owe them now, for all the stuff I bought.'

'Do you owe them?'

'They said I do,' Daria said, nodding.

'Daria, does Jamie ever seem a bit weird to you? Like, really angry? Like he hates everyone?'

She nodded. 'Yes. I think it's very hard for him.'

I wondered again about what exactly had happened in Daria's life that she was so completely blind about men. I felt some responsibility to help her out. I was sure I was wasting my time. 'Daria, what do you think is hard for him?'

'Well, you know, with Brad.'

She looked down, as if she was wondering if she should say anything. 'What about Brad? Brad is the nice one!'

She looked up suddenly, as if she couldn't stand to listen to such lies any more. I imagined she'd spent time watching herself in the mirror making that face – strong and loyal, defending her man. 'Jamie said that you would think that. He says that's what everyone thinks. Jamie says that he loves Brad like a brother and would never hear anyone say anything bad about him.'

'Have you got any cigarettes?'

Daria looked worried again. 'You shouldn't smoke, Faith, it's bad for you.'

'Tell me some more about what Jamie says.'

I figured that we might as well have it out. She wouldn't listen, but at least I'd know that I'd warned her. She took a deep breath. 'Jamie worries about Brad all the time, he's driven mad by the worry. It was Brad that got Jamie to start selling, and he wasn't sure it was a good idea, but he was a care worker and that was no good at all for him.'

Even trying really hard, I couldn't imagine Jamie being a good care worker. I could imagine Jamie punching an old man in the face and stealing his pension, or Jamie breaking into a retirement home, punching lots of people in the face and stealing the drugs, but I couldn't imagine him doing any kind of useful job at all. I told Daria that. She nodded, furiously, cheeks red. 'No! Because you see Jamie, and you just straight away think that he couldn't work in a shop, or at a nursery! Because you think he's not good enough. And,' she finished triumphantly, 'you hate men!'

I didn't laugh, because maybe she was right. It was true that I was usually pretty suspicious of men, but then that was mainly because they generally spent time trying to fuck me or get me to sell them good skunk too cheaply. Or, y'know, palming me off on their coke dealing friends. So, yeah, hands up, I find men annoying.

'Right. So Jamie wasn't cut out to look after old people?'

'It wasn't old people, actually. You'd know that if you'd ever made the effort to talk to him properly.'

'K.' I wasn't going to argue. I hadn't talked to Jamie properly. Hopefully I never would.

'And actually,' Daria paused, as if she was enjoying the moment, 'Brad got Jamie to help him, and then Brad got addicted to crack!'

She said it like that was a surprise. 'Poor Brad,' I said, without thinking.

Daria's leg was tapping away. I wondered what Jamie had been selling her. 'Poor Jamie! I couldn't tell you some of the stuff he's seen Brad do. It's disgusting, Faith.'

Now I wanted to know what disgusting things Brad did when he was high. Weed smokers are just generally less interesting, I guess. 'Wanking,' Daria hissed.

I shrugged. Men are disgusting. That seemed fairly standard. Daria was watching me, to see if I was impressed. 'And there was –' she stopped. 'I can't say, Faith. But I don't think Brad is a good man.'

That was strong, coming from Daria. 'So what are you doing here? If Brad is so disgusting?'

She closed her eyes again for a minute. 'Jamie says I need to drop a little bag off for them in some town up north, and then I can come home and we'll be all square, so that's all good, but what if Phil thinks I've gone off with Jamie?'

'Why would he think that?'

Daria's eyes got even bigger. 'Faith, I told him that! I didn't want him to know about the nice pills so I told him I was going round to Jamie's for a bit and then I told him I was staying the night! And then my phone got lost and Jamie said that he would text Phil and make it alright, but then he said he must have said *the wrong thing cos he said Phil was really mad with me and said not to come back! I know it's not his fault. Men are so bad at communicating.'*

'Right.'

'It will be okay though? Once I've paid Jamie back, I can explain to Phil? I love him.'

And then I couldn't be bothered to say anything to her. Which wasn't very nice, but I couldn't think of anything very nice to say. I couldn't even really be angry with her for being so gullible, because I was here too, waiting for my chance at the money. It was almost funny, how I'd been so happy to think Brad was looking out for me.

'All I have to do,' Daria said, nodding, 'is just deliver the parcel, and get the money and pay it back. Unless I want to do more, and get even more money, but I think I won't, not if Phil has stopped being mad.'

I had a feeling it wasn't going to be that easy. I was thinking that Jamie and Brad weren't like Phil and Jed with their nice friendly way of doing business, where you did your bit and then got paid, eventually. I had a feeling that Jamie and Brad were more the sort you heard about, who told you that you owed them again and again until you were stuck forever selling little bags to desperate people until you went to prison. Or got stabbed.

Angharad

Worcester looked terrifying to drive through but Jake didn't seem bothered, and hardly even had both hands on the wheel at the same time. I hoped that him being so relaxed meant he was a good driver.

He seemed fairly sure about the kind of place we were looking to stay and we drove around until he saw one he liked. It was called the White Horse, which seemed a bit surprising for a bed and breakfast. The paint was falling off the front door and one of the windows was smashed. I didn't understand why Jake was so sure that this was the best place in the whole of Worcester for us. It smelt like gravy and mashed potatoes and sweat, and the woman who opened the door had her slippers on. I nudged Jake. He looked at the slippers and then looked at me and rolled his eyes.

I shut up. It wasn't like I was the big expert on hotels.

I had thought Jake might expect us to share a bed. Me and Jake, lying on different sides of the same bed. But there were four beds. One of the beds was full of soft toys. Which was pretty surprising too. Though the owner did look exactly like the kind of woman who might think a bed covered in soft toys was a good idea.

Once he shut the door behind us, Jake dropped his bag on the floor. 'Don't start, Angharad,' he said.

I was going to cry again. Other teenagers didn't seem to cry whenever a man talked to them. Jake rummaged in his bag, pulled out a bar of chocolate and threw it at me. 'Time of the month,' he explained to me.

I wanted to argue, but I realised he was probably right. I ate the chocolate and ignored him smirking at me.

I was worried that Jake might expect us to drink wine or beer together. Or whatever people like him drank. I didn't think that would work out well for me. But Jake seemed more excited about getting pizza. So instead we walked down a street – busy even though it was nearly 11pm, looking for a pizza shop.

Jake was very definite that there would be one, and that it would be open. It seemed a bit unlikely to me. The takeaways at home were all shut up by 10, unless it was the Sheep Festival. I didn't mind walking around and looking though. Being in Worcester with Jake was completely different to being alone. I could see tower blocks in the distance and there was music playing, from someone's house or a pub. I felt like a tourist. In a good way. Not like someone unexpectedly caught up in something weird like last time. We stood and looked over a bridge at the canal below. It made me think of sitting with Daria. Jake must have been thinking about that too. 'I won't let anyone hurt you this time,' he said.

He was staring down at the dark water. I wasn't sure whether he meant to be as meaningful as he sounded. 'Okay.'

He nodded. 'Okay. Let's find the pizza.'

He grabbed my hand and led me off down the street. Just like Jake had predicted, we found one just a few metres along from the bridge. 'I bet you're a fucking vegetarian?'

I nodded, a bit embarrassed. Jake made a scoffing noise but he ordered a large vegetable one for us to share. While we were waiting for the pizza, I asked him about his weekend. 'Fuck's sakes, Angharad!'

I noticed that he used my full name when he was cross with me. Like my mum. Though I could never tell whether Jake was properly cross or just teasing. He looked at me, frowning. 'Sometimes you're just like all the other girlies.'

I felt a bit flattered. Sometimes he acted as if I was twelve instead of the same age as Ella, who he obviously didn't think of as a child.

'Like them but without the blowjobs?'

He laughed a lot at that. I liked how I could make him laugh. 'Yeah. Just the nagging. None of the good bits. The weekend was fine. Stop fishing.'

'I wasn't!'

That seemed unfair, when I'd just been chatting. Like a friend. I thought, anyway. I suppose I might have been just a little bit curious about what he did when he was away from me. Surely that was normal. Jake carried the pizza. We wandered back to the bridge and Jake opened the box and handed me a slice. I decided not to point out that we hadn't washed our hands. 'Shall I tell you what happened with Ella?' he asked. 'Give you one less thing to worry about?'

'I don't care.'

I crossed the road, fast. I knew he'd follow me, and he did, and caught up and grabbed my arm. He was laughing again. 'Okay, final time I'll offer. You know you want to know…'

I found I was laughing too. I did want to know. 'Go on, then. Tell me about your tragic love affair.'

He looked alarmed. 'It wasn't love! Jeez, Angh! Don't say that word! Especially not to her!'

'Okay, sorry.'

'Do you ever see her? Are you friends?'

I couldn't imagine anything less likely. 'She thinks I'm pathetic.'

He looked relieved. 'Oh, babe, you're not pathetic.' He looked thoughtful. 'You're just a bit up tight.'

I decided to change the subject from my failings. I suspected if Jake got going he had loads of things he could tell me I was bad at. And I wanted to ask him how old Ella was. And if she was sixteen, whether that made it okay for him to be seeing her.

'Go on, Jake, tell me what happened. I won't talk to her, I hardly ever even see her and she's not my friend.'

I leaned back against the bridge wall, and he leant next to me. He was so tall. 'Okay. Well, I thought she was really nice, and cool.'

I translated that in my head as 'keen to have sex with me

and didn't mind if I didn't reply to her texts'. I felt like I was starting to understand Jake. 'Yeah? And then what happened?'

'She just started hassling me all the time about what I was doing and who I was seeing. Like we were married or something. And getting pissy about it. Like telling you that I was with Faith.'

He shrugged. I could understand how frustrating Jake would be if you thought there was a chance you might actually be his girlfriend and he wasn't as interested as you were. I decided to try even harder not to ask him too many questions about where he was when he wasn't with me. 'So you're not seeing her any more?'

'Well, not really. Just sometimes, you know.'

I didn't know.

Faith

It was getting late when Jamie came back. It was dark outside, and Daria was asleep again. She was dribbling, but it was kind of cute. I was sitting watching her, thinking sadly about vodka and cigarettes and wondering why I didn't fancy nice, pretty, gullible Daria. Whatever she said, I was pretty sure that with a bit of encouraging she'd be putty in my hand.

Jamie had brought vodka, but his mouth was tight in a way that didn't look good. He got straight to the point. Didn't say anything, just stood over me, looking down as if he was still thinking about how badly I wrapped crack. I bet Jamie wouldn't stop me listening to Eminem because it was sexist. Jamie probably thought Eminem should treat people a bit meaner, teach them their place. Especially women.

I sat and waited. I didn't think saying anything would help, right now. I was waiting for him to touch me, but I wasn't expecting it would be with his foot. It wasn't a proper kick, but it hurt. And it was weird, being kicked. Even though a lot of people think I'm shit, I don't think I've ever been kicked before. I wanted to look away, but I was scared to. I wished Brad would come back. Or Daria would wake up and distract him.

'I don't like you,' he said.

No big surprise there, but I don't think anyone had ever said that to my face, either. Not even at school. The good thing about hanging out with two dodgy pot sellers is that when you're thirteen, you look pretty cool and even if everyone was bitching, they were too scared to do it to my face.

Jamie kicked me again, harder. I needed to think of something to do, a way to stop him, but my brain wasn't working fast enough.

'Did you hear me?' he said, pushing his foot into my ribs.

I wanted to tell him that I didn't like him either, because he was a dick. But I just curled up. I didn't know how far he'd go, but I guessed he probably wouldn't kill me. And that's the bottom line.

After he got bored with pushing at me with his foot, Jamie knelt down in front of me. 'You're pathetic,' he said, not shouting, just telling me.

And he was right. I was stuck in this flat, with a bloke who seemed to spend a lot of time wanting to hurt me, and who seemed to be the sort of drug dealer that give drug dealers a bad name. Turned out there was a reason teachers were always banging on about drugs being bad and gangs being bad. It had all seemed a lot more fun when I was in the gang and taking the drugs. This wasn't my sort of gang. I had thought it might be, but it definitely wasn't. It didn't seem like it was Daria's either really, but I wasn't sure what I could do about that. I wanted her to wake up, so I wasn't here alone, with Jamie, but if he was going to be hitting someone it might as well be me.

He grabbed my arm and stood up, pulling me with him. His fingers dug into my bare skin. I'd been thinking maybe he wouldn't want me covered in bruises, but he didn't seem to be worried. He pushed me back, until I was against the wall. We stood there. It felt like he was getting ready for something, gearing himself up.

And at first, I was just going to let it happen. I was hungry and scared and bored, and he was tall and horrible and a lot stronger than me. No one was going to come and rescue me. And then I thought about little Angharad, poking around, asking questions, getting me shut in this shitty flat. And for the first time in my entire life, ever, it felt a bit like someone might be on my side. And like I owed her to at least try to get away from this.

I grabbed his middle finger and yanked it back. It was something a bouncer had shown me. Jamie yelped and was about to bring his other hand round to hit me, but before he got going I used my other hand to punch him as hard as I could in the balls, and instead of hitting me his hand clutched at his groin.

I was terrified, but quite impressed with myself too. It was too late to stop, so I stood up and ran to the door. It was locked. Obviously.

I'd been hoping hard that Jamie had forgotten to lock it. I looked back at him. He was standing up, still clutching himself and looking seriously pissed off. He was fucking massive standing up.

I could feel myself starting to lose it and focused everything on just keeping it together. I needed something to hit him with. Something good. I ran back to the kitchen units. If I could find a knife… I wished I'd looked properly earlier when I had time. I could hear Jamie coming towards me. I scrabbled through the top drawer, hoping I'd see something – anything. I could hear him panting, getting nearer. 'You bitch.'

His breath was on my face. I grabbed at the forks and threw them at his face, then pulled myself up onto the worktop. His face was red and furious and his mouth was stretched wide, snarling like a dog.

I grabbed the massive swanky copper frying pan from where it sat on the hob. It was heavier than it looked. Before I could think too much, I lamped him hard on the head with it, from up on the worktop. I did it again and again, as hard as I could. I'm not that strong, but I was really fucking scared. I wasn't thinking, just hitting and hitting, like hammering a nail in.

He was on his knees before I saw the keys. Sitting on the worktop, near the fridge. I grabbed them and legged it to the door, still carrying the pan even though my wrist was hurting. I fumbled trying to get the key in because I was trying to watch him too, but I got there before he got back up. I pulled the door open, threw the pan back at him and ran. I didn't let myself think about Daria.

I had passed the fire door before I realised the lift would be a bad idea. I went back, opened the door, and there were concrete stairs and not much else. I ran down a couple of flights and then stopped to see if I could hear anything. I really didn't want to be trapped here if Brad was coming up. It was silent.

I carried on running, down the stairs and out into the lobby, then out into the night. I ran down to the canal. Stopped in front of Journey's End, its shadow hanging across the path. Felt like my breath had stopped in my throat. Realised I still didn't know where Brad was. Started running again. I stopped under the first bridge. I didn't even have my coat. I was already missing my coat. It would have meant I was further away from the shitty old rest of the world. I touched the old red bricks by my side, back from when the canals were built. They were still warm from the day. Further along, I could see a light, I guessed on a boat. I headed towards it. I really wanted to just curl up next to the bricks and sleep but I figured it was sensible to keep moving. I didn't know what time it was, but it was almost dark. Not a great time to be wandering around alone down here, but it seemed unlikely that anything worse could happen.

I passed the boat and kept moving. There were kids' bikes on the roof, so hopefully a nice dad might come and help if I screamed. I decided it was best to get right away from the flats. There was no one around as I walked. I wasn't completely sure I was going towards the centre, but Worcester isn't huge and I figured I'd get there eventually. I was pretty pleased with myself. Hitting some bloke on the head with a frying pan was fucking awesome. I was grinning to myself a bit as I walked. No coat and no money and no phone, but I was out of that flat and away from sweaty, dodgy men. For now anyway. I suspected some would turn up again at some point. They usually do.

Angharad

We finished the pizza and stayed on the bridge. I was leaning over the wall, looking down at the water. There weren't many people about on the street now. I wondered if Jake was going to kiss me, and if he was, would it be tonight? I thought about what he'd asked in the car. Did I want to kiss him? I peered sideways at him. He was still stubbly. I wasn't sure how that would feel.

He was looking at me. My stomach felt tense. He smiled. 'You know Cerys and Sue are gays?'

'What?'

He put his arm around me. 'Cerys and Sue, from your church.'

He rubbed his arm up and down. 'Angh, you're very tense. You should relax a bit.'

I put my hand on his, to stop the rubbing, which was annoying when I was trying to concentrate. 'Cerys? Are you sure?'

He looked at me. 'Welcome to the real world, sweetie.'

'Why would I know? I'm not their friend. They're old.'

I felt so ignorant. Why hadn't I noticed, if Jake had? Why had nobody told me? Did everyone in Llanyfenni know? Did they know about me? Jake started rubbing again. I tried to remember seeing Cerys and Sue together, to remember what they had been doing. They were always together, I realised, or smiling at each other, or arriving together or getting each other cups of tea. Jake was stroking more than rubbing now, but still talking. 'Nice old things. Bring their car in. Old Saab. No electrics on it, all proper old mechanics. Lovely. Diesel, too.'

I rubbed my eyes, in case I was going to cry. Jake was stroking my back now. He had turned sideways, to face me. He seemed to be waiting for me to say something. I was still thinking. He sounded awkward. 'I just worry, you know, that you'll end up like that.'

'What?'

'Well, old. Messy hair. No kids. And probably never been kissed, properly, by a man. It's tragic for them, really.'

There were swans, down on the water. I wondered if swans went to bed. I realised I was very tired and probably that's why I felt like crying again. 'You're very pretty, Angharad,' Jake said, putting his other arm across me so he could turn me around to face him.

We were very close. I kept looking down, at the button on his jeans. I knew he must still be looking at me, and it was all too much. I was crying again, and he put his arms around me and even though it felt wrong, I let him hug me and snivelled into his t-shirt and breathed in his lovely deodorant and leather and sweat smell and felt his strong arms round me and for a few minutes I pretended that he was my boyfriend and would look after me and that everything was fine.

Faith

I kept walking. I stayed by the canal. I figured they were more likely to follow me in a car, and if they came this way at least I'd probably hear them. Walking gave me time to think.

All this time I'd been laughing at them. I thought I had them wrapped round my finger, paying for my cute new phone and my funky Vans and the gas bill. And it was like taking sweets from a baby, selling in Llanyfenni. Nodding and smiling and handing out my little bags 24/7.

When I was a kid, my dad bought me a PlayStation. I was only seven, too young to know that nothing ever turns out right. He pawned it a few weeks later, along with the games I'd borrowed from a girl at school. She made me pay her back for what they'd been worth new, in instalments. Never saw the PS again. That's been my entire life, stuff like that, one thing after another so I'd been pretty thick not to wonder why guys were stuffing money in my pocket and all I had to do was answer texts all day and all night and hand out weed. I'd missed something, if they were so stressed about me stopping.

And whatever had gone on in the flat wasn't nice. However flash the flat looked, I was pretty sure some bad shit happened there. Having hobnobs and letting kids hang out in your flat didn't actually mean you were a good person. The more I thought about it, the more I thought that it might be the sort of thing you did if you were a very bad person. I dug my fingers into my wrist. Told myself just to keep walking.

I walked past a line of boats, all tied in a tidy line bobbing cheerfully. Nice little narrow boats, not like Jamie's boat. There were rings on the path but they were easy enough to walk around. No lights on these boats. I guess they were all tucked up in bed. Some of them had those red and white striped life-ring things on the roof, for if someone fell in. Most of them had wheelbarrows. Made sense I guess, though you'd look like a right fool walking through Worcester with your wheelbarrow. They had big long poles. Fuck knows what they were for. And little flower pots full of herbs. And watering cans.

It must be nice just going wherever you want, all around the country, away from everyone. I imagined Angharad and I on a tiny boat, her in an apron stirring something on a teeny tiny stove. Cute. Obviously I was being ridiculous. I just wanted to see her again.

Angharad

When I stopped crying, I looked up at Jake, to see if it was going to be awkward. He was looking down at me. Ages ago I read a book, and it said that if you really wanted someone (a boy, I guess the book meant) to kiss you, you should stand close to him and look up (it seemed to assume it would be a tall boy), and he wouldn't be able to help himself. And I realised that was how it felt. I was standing looking up, and Jake was staring down at me as if I was as sexy and beautiful as Ella. And there was a funny feeling inside my stomach, and suddenly I could imagine that just maybe, being in bed with Jake might be very, very nice. And then I panicked. 'Look at the swans,' I said, turning away.

Jake didn't look at the swans, he was still watching me. I kept looking down, wanting him to look away and hoping that he didn't. 'Angharad –' he said, and then stopped.

I waited, holding my breath. He said, 'Look at the stars.'

I looked where he was pointing. They weren't as bright as at home. He stood behind me so I could see where he was pointing, his arm on my shoulder. 'That's Venus, over there,' he said, and I could hear the smile in his voice.

Even when he stopped pointing, he didn't move away. He was so close that I could feel him all the way down my body. I didn't move.

I wished I had just let him kiss me and got it over with. I looked down at the boats. They were very sweet, all tied up in a tidy little line. In the street lights you could see the effort people had put into making them nice, with all their gleaming painted sides and flower pots and painted watering cans. There was someone down in the shadows, leaning against the wall, staring at them too. They weren't moving. Drunk, I figured, and turned back to look at Jake.

'Come on then, girlie,' he said, and we walked off back to the strange White Horse.

Faith

I'd got it wrong. Again. I should have realised that they weren't just going to let me go. I should have run when I had the chance. I would have kicked myself but I was pretty sure Jamie would do that for me soon enough.

I didn't even hear them coming, I was so busy staring at boats and daydreaming. 'Come on, little Faith,' Brad said, looming at me out of the shadows.

'Time to come home,' Jamie said. I could hear the smile in his voice.

I swore and just took off, as fast as I could. I didn't look round. Just ran. I could hear them chasing me, their feet were thumping down on the dry ground. I didn't stop, just did the running I should have done earlier, as if running could put right all the mistakes I'd made.

My heart was banging in my chest, and my mouth was dry. I couldn't remember the last time I'd drunk anything apart from coffee. It didn't take long before I realised I was going to lose them. I was fast and scared and they were just idiots who messed around in the gym. If one of them actually punched me, they'd probably break my jaw, but as long as I just kept running they wouldn't get the chance.

So I kept on running, pounding along the side of the canal on the dusty path. I ran round corners and under bridges and over train lines. After a while I couldn't hear them, but I kept going anyway. I'd screwed up once by stopping, I wasn't going to screw up again. And it felt good to run.

There was no one else around down here — the city was all up above my head. I could hear the cars and the odd bit of music and shouting but whatever time it was, things were quietening down. I was scared to stop in the end. I had this irrational feeling that as long as I was running it'd be okay. So I carried on running.

Angharad

We sat up on the double bed together, watching TV. Which was a novelty for me, because my parents didn't have one. We did have Netflix, I wasn't completely unfamiliar with the idea of moving pictures on a screen or anything. But Marriage Bootcamp and Don't Tell the Bride and Through the Keyhole with a man who seemed to spend a lot of his time in tight gold pants was new.

Looking for Faith was more fun with Jake. I had almost stopped worrying about actually finding her, because looking for her was so much fun. I liked watching Jake. I especially liked watching Jake when he smiled, or moved around and you could see his muscles moving under his t-shirt. I also liked that he didn't seem to think I was weird. Well, he did, but not that weird, or at least weird but funny. And he didn't seem scared by the idea of going to tackle Jed in the morning. I was so scared when I thought about that that it was hard to breathe. Thinking about Faith was complicated but Jake was complicated in a familiar sort of way. Everyone knew boys were weird and didn't like to commit and you had to learn special ways to talk to them. I was starting to feel like a conversation with Jake was more like chess than I'd realised. Or like chess when the rules kept changing. Just like it should be.

I was a bit irritated by the way that Jake never seemed to be able to stick to an arrangement, but I guessed I didn't really know what having a job – two jobs – was like. I realised I didn't even actually know where he lived. I didn't want to spoil things by asking him things that he might think were trying to pin him down.

So we sat watching crap television until I realised I was falling asleep next to him. I might not have noticed, if he hadn't woken me up. 'Babe, you're falling asleep.'

But he didn't really seem to mind, so I let my eyes shut

again and after a few minutes I heard him sigh loudly and pull the blanket out from under me and then get up and walk round the bed. I lay there while he pulled my legs down the bed. He was muttering something about bad, lazy girls but he didn't sound angry. He flopped the blanket back over me and then climbed back into bed on the other side and sat back up. After a few minutes I heard him laughing to himself at the television.

I woke up in the night lying close to him. Still in my clothes. And I hadn't brushed my teeth. I lay for a few minutes with my eyes shut, trying to get back to sleep. In the dark, next to Jake Morgan. I wanted to enjoy it. Maybe this was how it was supposed to feel if you really liked someone. Jake turned over, and threw one of his arms over me. I felt myself go tense. I tried to relax. It was just an arm. I tried to pretend that it wasn't too heavy and hairy and that Jake wasn't too close, but I couldn't breathe.

I pushed my way out from under his arm, and out of the blanket, and across the room. It was dark, and I couldn't tell where the other bed was. I bashed my toe on something. It really hurt. I clambered into the first bed I came to. It was the one with the freaky toys. Of course. I wriggled under the blanket, and under the toys, feeling most of them fall off. Which was probably for the best. 'Night, Angharad,' Jake said, sounding like he was laughing again.

Faith

When the sky finally started turning red in the distance I felt better. My mum loves the sunrise. She used to wake me up, back when I was a kid, and hold me up by the window to see it. It was like our special time. Whoever else was in the house, when she woke me up it was just us two, looking out at the world. Then a few years back, when I was still trying to go to school, it was all too much. I went mad at her about it. I was just shouting and screaming about just wanting to sleep.

And that's when I started going out at night. It was better than thinking I might lose it with her. I hated seeing her face drop and her eyes get teary. My poor mum, she didn't want much, and I screwed it up. I walked while the street lights turned off and the planes started crossing the sky and the boats started shifting about as if people were moving inside.

I found a bench in a park and sat. There were a lot of people walking through – going to work, I guess. It felt fairly safe. People tried not to look at me when they passed me. I knew why. I was still wearing my dress, which had looked pretty good forty-eight hours ago, but probably not so good now. I hadn't looked in a mirror for a while but my face felt dirty and I could see my hands were.

I was really hungry, but I couldn't think of much that I could do about that for now. I could sort my face a bit, I decided, and found some public toilets over by the pond. They were grim and the sink was tiny but it felt better afterwards. I was almost too scared to leave the toilets. I had to force myself to peer out, like some little fluffy animal on a nature programme. Like prey, I thought.

I remembered the way Phil had been in Wetherspoons. I should have known then. I wasn't part of the big money making venture, I was just a disposable kid needing pulled into shape. Or punched into shape. Whatever it took, I guessed. I wondered what normal teenagers would do in this situation. They'd have someone they could ask to help though, I thought. Someone useful. I decided to go and see my dad.

Angharad

Jake woke me up by having a shower, singing something that sounded like Yma o Hyd very loudly and then, in case I was still thinking I might get back to sleep, by making a lot of noise getting dressed. I looked at my phone. It was nearly ten o'clock. I was surprised that I'd slept so late. Jake was looking all fresh from the shower, standing in his pants, brushing his teeth. I carefully looked up at his face, trying to ignore the naked parts of him. And the pant-clad bits, which were very close to my face. 'Good morning,' I said.

I was trying to sound cheery and casual, as if I was used to almost-naked men brushing their teeth by my bed. I didn't know why he couldn't just brush them in the bathroom. Wasn't it normal to brush your teeth in the bathroom?

'Morning, Angharad,' he said, around his toothbrush.

Even with toothpaste dribbling down his chin he looked cute. I shut my eyes in case I accidentally saw the shape of his penis through his pants. Practised saying cock inside my head, like the Home Ed girls did. Desensitizing myself, like it was a spider. Wondered if Jake would be on board with a gradual programme of getting used to his genitals.

He loped off back to the bathroom. I could hear him spitting and rinsing and washing. Oh, and then peeing. This was all far too much. I didn't hear him turning the tap on. Didn't he wash his hands? Was that normal? He came bouncing back out into the bedroom. I couldn't help it. 'Don't forget to wash your hands, Jake.'

He made a face and went back in. I wondered if all boys were this annoying. All people. How did anyone manage to stay married for forty years? Did you just have to put up with them until you stopped noticing? Or could you teach them to be less disgusting? He bounced back out again and yanked the curtains open. 'Sun's shining,' he said.

'Cool.'

I wondered if it would make me look as uptight as people kept telling me I was if I took my clean clothes into the bathroom to get dressed. Or re-dressed seeing as I'd never got undressed last night. My teeth felt horrible. 'Come on, Angh, I'm starving.'

I got ready as quickly as I could. In the bathroom, because I didn't see how I could put my clean jeans on without bending over and I didn't want Jake looking at me or saying anything. I suspected he'd seen a lot of girls putting their jeans on and I didn't want him comparing me in his head. Or out loud. Or offering helpful tips about a sexier way of doing it and I wasn't sure he'd be able to resist that.

Jake told the woman at the desk – which was more of a skanky table covered in those circle stains mugs make – that we'd keep the room for the night. 'Just in case,' he said.

I wasn't sure if my nerves could cope with another night alone with Jake. But at least he was thinking about it. He must like me a bit, I thought. Must not think of me as a total child. Must want to spend time with me, as if I was like Ella.

The White Horse wasn't the kind of place that did breakfast. 'So it's not really a bed and breakfast at all,' I pointed out to Jake.

He rolled his eyes. He drove around looking for a McDonald's for a bit. I thought it would be more sensible to drive and park near the station because there was probably one near there, in the middle of town, but Jake seemed to think that was a bizarre idea so I shut up.

We found one in the end. 'Ha!' Jake said, as if that proved something other than that if you drive around for long enough you can find anything.

I wasn't even convinced that we were in Worcester any more. 'So we'll go to Wetherspoons and see if we can find this Jamie?' I said.

Jake's mouth was full of burger. He nodded. He had

mayonnaise on his chin. I passed him a serviette. He looked like he was thinking hard. 'It's funny that he's called Jamie and I'm Jake,' he said, eventually.

'Mm.' I wasn't sure what he wanted me to say, so I moved on. 'How will we get him to tell us where Faith is?'

Jake finished chewing. 'I reckon we'll just figure it out once we get there.'

He rubbed my hair affectionately. I hoped there wasn't mayonnaise on his hand. It was lucky that the more time I spent with Jake the easier it got to stop noticing how beautiful he was and the harder it got not to notice he was quite annoying. And a bit dirty. But it was definitely very nice not being on my own.

So we parked the car in a huge car park with lots of floors and went to the Wetherspoons, which turned out to be called The Old Bank, and not Journey's End at all. I had thought that might mean that there was no point going in, but apparently we might as well, seeing as we were there. Jake ordered a pint and I had an orange juice. We sat in a corner so I could watch in case the scary white trainer men turned up. 'If they do, I could stop them seeing your face by kissing you,' Jake said, looking deep into my eyes.

I held my breath. I didn't know what to say, so I just looked back. We stared at each other. 'I really like you,' he said.

And I realised that however disgusting and annoying he was, I was fooling myself if I pretended he wasn't gorgeous. I tried to think about it objectively, as if he was a beautiful tree or a waterfall or something. I still didn't know what to say. He nodded and then looked away, sipping his pint.

I was sure it was a bit early to be drinking alcohol, but he wasn't the only one in there with a pint. Maybe lots of people started drinking lager at lunchtime. We didn't see the men with the white trainers, or anyone that looked like they might steal someone's phone or have a bad aura.

Jake was keen to get another pint, but I couldn't see how that would help. It felt like he was getting a bit narky with me but it could have been the other way around. In the end he said he could go to Phil's and see if he could find out anything. I wasn't sure that was very sensible, when the men had been so angry with me for doing pretty much the same thing. 'I won't even mention Faith, don't worry. And to be honest, you're boring me, Angharad,' Jake said, getting up and striding off.

I wondered what the point of him going was if he wasn't going to mention Faith. Then suddenly I wondered if Jake was less interested in Faith than in buying weed. I stood up to follow him then sat back down. Bloody Jake, who had been very reassuring about looking after me and then disappeared and left me almost exactly where I'd been attacked. Bloody, bloody, bloody Jake, I thought. Hunting for Faith was definitely making me swear a lot more. I phoned him but, predictably, he didn't answer.

I sat, alone, in a pub I'd never been in before, where I knew some dodgy bloke might turn up at any minute, with hardly any money, and no idea where the White Horse even was.

So I got myself a drink. I wasn't sure what else I was supposed to do. I thought the bar staff would ask me for some sort of ID, and had decided if they did, that would be a sign (possibly from God, finally joining in a bit) and I would walk away. But they didn't seem interested in my age. I asked for half a Stella, because it had a pretty name and I wasn't sure if a whole pint would be too much. I took it to a different table, far enough from the bar that hopefully a manager wouldn't wander in and notice that a fifteen year old was drinking. I also wanted to be far enough from the street that the police wouldn't see me. I'd never been an underage drinker before and I wasn't sure how much the police would care. Swearing and drinking and sleeping near men. Arguing with my mum. I was definitely crossing some teen goals off my list.

I kept watching for someone who might be Jamie. I didn't know what I was going to do if I saw him, but probably hide in the toilets. I kept drinking slowly. It turned out I didn't like lager.

She had short dark hair, shaved up the sides. She was tall and straight. She was walking round collecting glasses in a green plastic box thing. I wondered how old you had to be to do that job. I was thinking I probably needed a job too. She didn't look much older than me. I was starting to realise that what felt like a lot of pocket money six months ago wasn't anything like enough at the moment. And Jake had paid for the White Horse, I realised. And the petrol. And the pizza. I felt guilty. I checked to see if he'd tried to call, but he hadn't.

I drank some more lager and started thinking about the future, once this was finished and I was back in Llanyfenni. I couldn't live with my parents not doing any exams and hanging out by myself forever. I wondered if feeling like your life was pointless and you did nothing interesting ever was depression or just normal if you were a teenager. If I had a friend, I could ask them.

When the girl got to my table, she smiled down at me. 'Alright?'

She sounded like Faith too. I smiled back. When I finished my drink, I decided I might as well get another one. The first few gulps had been a bit grim, but by the last few I felt it had potential. The girl was serving. Her badge said her name was Kim. She handed me the glass without saying anything.

I went back to my table. By the time I sat down, I was wishing I'd asked for orange juice. I was feeling a bit odd. I watched as another girl walk up to the bar. Kim was smiling at her and the girl was smiling back. They were laughing about something together. I tried not to stare enviously.

Apart from the day at the steam rally with Faith, I hadn't really had the kind of life that included laughing with friends. I stopped drinking the lager and let it sit on the table. If I was going to try and be a better teenager with a social life and friends, sitting alone in Wetherspoons drinking lager all afternoon wasn't a good start.

In a book, the girls at the bar might have included me and we'd have all ended up great buddies. Instead, I just sat waiting patiently for Jake and hoping no one came to the pub and tried to hurt me. I did notice when Kim left with the girl from the bar. They were holding hands. I watched as they walked passed the big windows and stopped to cross the road. Their heads were close together and I realised they were kissing.

I wasn't sure I'd ever seen girls kissing in real life. Real life, especially in Llanyfenni, isn't exactly like Netflix. Unless Jake was right about Sue and Cerys. I accidentally imagined them, naked, wrapped around each other. I couldn't help thinking about what Jake had said, about me ending up like Cerys and Sue. Running the lunch club and helping the homeless. Hanging out with the people in the congregation that everyone else thought were too weird. Laughing and smiling together. I sat and watched, my head on my hands. Just knowing there were places in the world where girls could kiss each other in the street, without even caring, made the whole world seem a friendlier place.

More and more men came into Wetherspoons as the afternoon went on. But I knew when the two white trainer men came in because my stomach went weird and my whole body started shaking. I hadn't factored that in when I'd decided I could just go and hide in the toilet. My knees were shaking too much to even think about standing up.

The men weren't talking to each other, and neither of them looked happy. They stood at the bar with a pint each. One of them looked like he had a black eye. I took a careful sip, trying to blend in. I knew if they looked at me that they couldn't help but recognise me, though they had seemed like they might be the kind of people who did a lot of that sort of thing. Maybe all the scared people blurred into one.

I kept looking down. I didn't know what I was going to do. It was surely only a matter of time before they saw me. My hands were so shaky I had to let go of the glass. I forced myself to sit up, because all I wanted to do was curl up under the table and close my eyes. I needed to look up, to see what they were doing, but I couldn't.

I felt someone coming towards me. I still couldn't look up. 'Babe,' Jake said.

He swung himself down into the chair opposite me. I was still shaking. I looked up at him, into his eyes. 'Jeez, Angharad, you're not sulking, are you?'

'Jake –' I said.

I heard how breathless I sounded, like some pathetic heroine in a film. 'Jake –' I started again.

He looked at me, one eyebrow up. 'They're there. The men. Don't look!' I added as his head started to swing around.

'Which men?'

'The men that chased me by the station. Before. They're by the bar. I'm scared.'

He looked at me. 'They didn't really chase you though, did they?' he said, then finally noticed how scared I was. 'Oh, babe.'

'What if they see me?'

'Bring your chair round, next to mine.'

I did, and he put his arm round me. I leant against him, feeling his warmth. He smelt of weed. I didn't really want to think about what that meant. I just sat leaning and waiting to calm down. 'They've finished their pints. They're going,' Jake updated me.

I nodded and Jake poked at me, 'Come on, then, let's follow them,'

'Follow them?'

This seemed like a very bad idea. 'Yes, come on,' Jake jumped to his feet, 'Quick, Angh, we'll lose them.'

I really, really hoped we would, but followed him obediently out of the pub. Anything was better than being left there on my own again. I couldn't understand why Jake was so keen to be face-to-face with them, unless he just hadn't listened to literally anything I'd said about them and how scary they were. I was worried. I was pretty sure if they saw us, Jake would end up lying on the floor all mashed up and bleeding in a doorway. Even if they hadn't been following me, they both looked like they might do that kind of thing for fun. Jake was charging after them like an eager puppy. They were marching off down the street. 'Come on, come on!' Jake was pulling me along.

I let myself be dragged, hoping that they wouldn't see us, or if they did that at least they wouldn't be able to do much to two of us in broad daylight in the middle of a city. Then I realised Jake was enthusiastically dragging me down a narrow, dark alley. I could see water gleaming in the sunlight at the bottom of it. I dug my heels in, literally. 'No, Jake!'

He turned back to me. 'We've nearly got them!'

'What if they're waiting at the bottom?'

'I fucking hope they are!'

'I'm scared!'

Jake was staring furiously at me. 'Babe, you're with me, come on!'

'But Jake –' I didn't know how to get him to understand.

Jake let go of my hand. 'Come on, then. Best do what you think, Angharad. Seeing as you know so much about everything.'

I was crying. Again. I was so fed up of every conversation with Jake being so hard. And so fed up of being scared. We walked back up to the street and to the car. Jake was marching ahead and I was trailing behind, snot dribbling down my face. People were looking at me, but no one said anything. So it was fine for girls to kiss girls in Worcester, but fine as well to shout at girls until they cried and then walk off. At home, I knew someone would have pushed a tissue into my hand, even if they were also asking me a load of questions about what had happened. Home felt a long way away.

Brad

So Faith has ruined everything. Little bitch.

Faith

I wasn't completely sure when I'd last seen my dad. My mum and I usually tried to pretend he didn't exist, though sometimes if she was drunk she'd tell me about when they first met, and he had money and a car and a job and used to bring her flowers. I suspected that lasted right up until she got pregnant with Steven about three months later. I haven't met my brother; he was taken into care pretty soon after he was born.

I try not to think about how much worse things must have been at home then. He's two years older than me. I know his birthday because it's always a bad day for my mum. I try to make sure I look after her. Take her a cup of tea without bitching, make sure she eats. There's not much else I can do really. She blames herself for him being taken away and she's probably right.

The social workers were round all the time when I was little, and my mum was really trying. I guess she was older the second time around and she didn't have my dad around so much. It must have been easier without him, because they didn't take me. They kept telling her if she got it together she might get my brother back but she never did. I don't even know if she saw him. It's hard to imagine my mum managing to rock up at some location at the right time and date for some kind of supervised visit. She's not great at that kind of thing. She's more likely to have panicked and had a few drinks instead. She's not great with pressure.

She doesn't talk much about Steven, or about the bit when my dad appeared again two years later with his big promises about a future together, got drunk with her, punched her in the face and got her pregnant with me. My mum still talks about him like he's her true love, when she talks about him at all. It's not like there haven't been plenty of other men in my mum's life. But it's my dad she is waiting for. When she mentions getting pregnant with me, it's like the punching was a minor

"

blip on their road to true love. A way she knew he cared, because she was the one he came to at the end of the night. Once a year or so, if he could be bothered to stagger his way across town.

When I was little, he'd phone now and again and say he was coming round. My mum would be trying to dress me up like one of those catalogue model kids. She couldn't, because my clothes were all either too big or too small or not really my clothes at all. Even as a kid, I'd known I wasn't pulling it off. I'd have my hair in ribbons except we didn't have ribbons so it'd be string or that stiff shiny stuff you wrap round Christmas presents. It didn't matter anyway because nine times out of ten my dad wouldn't turn up, or he'd be so late my mum would have started drinking and crying and forgotten all about me.

When he did actually turn up, my dad was nice to me. He'd sit me on his knee and tell me I was a princess and his special girl and he'd do anything for me. All that sort of stuff. It took me years to realise it was all bollocks.

The way she tells it, they're destined to be together and one day he'll come to his senses and come to her on his knees begging forgiveness. I don't point out he could barely get it together to get a taxi for twenty minutes down the road. Anyway. Mainly we don't talk about him, because it's depressing for both of us.

So he owed me, and I was calling some of it in. I wanted something to eat at least and a bit of cash. If that was asking too much, one or the other would do.

I didn't know for sure where he was living, but I was pretty sure I knew where he'd be drinking, and he was. Sitting up at the bar with his back to me but I could tell it was him. The bar maid was listening to him looking like she thought he was god's gift. Well, that's what she was aiming for, and she was pretty good, but I've been there myself often enough to tell that she was faking it. She probably had to listen to his shit every afternoon and pretending to be interested in his next big plan and how he was getting his life together now must have got boring. 'Dad,' I said firmly.

I wanted to save us both the embarrassment of him not recognising me. He took a minute to turn around. I wasn't offended. To be fair to him, after a few moments of looking blank, he did seem pleased to see me. The barmaid looked pretty relieved too. He told her to get me a vodka and coke, which was almost a nice thought. We had an awkward hug. He smelt like a wet jumper left in a corner. It was weirdly reassuring. Some things don't change and, sadly, my dad was one of them.

I asked if he'd buy me something to eat too, while he was still doing his impression of a good dad, so he threw in some prawn cocktail crisps. Also not what I wanted, but I ate them in two seconds, and listened to my dad explaining that he'd been just about to call me and he would have been over but he's been so busy with this new business idea that was really going to sort him out and then he'd be able to help me out. He'd even buy me a car, he said, nodding at me sincerely. I didn't remind him that I was only fifteen. It didn't seem worth ruining his happy dream.

When he started from the beginning again, with his big plans, I interrupted to ask him if he could lend me some money. He was delighted at the idea, but didn't have any spare on him right now. If I came back tomorrow he could definitely get me some. 'Bloody kids, always after my dough,' he said cheerily, looking round for someone to witness how put upon he was.

The barmaid had taken advantage of me taking up my dad's attention to disappear out to the back of the bar. I didn't blame her at all, I'd only been there ten minutes and already he was getting boring. I didn't pay much attention when she came back around, until she dumped a ham sandwich and a glass of water down in front of me. I looked up at her. She winked. 'Eat it. I'll put it on his tab.'

She said, more loudly, 'Paul, your daughter's starving. I've made her a sandwich and put it on your tab. You need to look after her better.'

My dad laughed, to show how much of a joke we were all

having. I thought I might cry so I just nodded at the barmaid, hoping I looked as grateful as I felt, and then I ate it. Obviously it was fucking awesome. And the water. I figured I'd got pretty much all the help I was likely to get from my dad. It would have been nice to have a different kind of dad, but this was mine. It was kind of nice to see him and realise that he was completely shit and I never ever had to see him again.

While I was there, I nipped to the toilet, had a slightly better wash – warm water and everything – and on the way back to the bar snaffled a steak knife from a plate on one of the tables. It seemed rude when the barmaid had been so nice but I couldn't stop remembering how much I'd wished I had one back at that flat. It was grubby, with blood or gravy, I wasn't sure. I gave my dad a hug goodbye for old times' sake, and went back out into the hot afternoon.

Mr Thomas

The weather had gone back to relentlessly hot. On a Thursday, I often visit the 'straying flock'. That's a little joke. It's what I like to call the members of the congregation who need a little extra support. With the uncertainty created by Marie and her daughter, I felt that it would be worth visiting Cerys for a chat. Marie seems to think some teenager is coming to stay with her. And that is the last thing we need – more of Marie's teenagers in Llanyfenni. It is always hard to discourage people from coming to church, but there comes a point where I must protect the congregation from contamination.

Cerys lives up outside the town, on a hill past the rugby club. By the time I walked up there, I wished that I had driven. I paused to admire the view. Cerys's cottage was certainly well-located.

Her garden gate was open, despite the chickens roaming all over the garden. The lawn needed cutting and her bushes appeared to be unkempt. It was the first time I had visited in years and it took me a moment to decide whether to use the back door. Pausing on the lawn, I caught sight of Cerys. She was just inside the large picture window, sitting at an easel. I moved to see what she was painting. It turned out to be Sue, who was spread-eagled across the bed. With no clothes on at all.

I pray for them.

Angharad

Jake wouldn't speak to me all the way back to the White Horse. I was angry with myself and with him, but I wanted to know what had happened with Phil. In the end I apologised for being so scared. He looked at me as if he was looking at dog shit. Then he sighed and slammed into the bathroom. I sat on the floor by his bed. I couldn't be bothered not to cry any more. I was very tired and hungry and I hated Jake and Faith was still missing and my head was hurting again.

And I probably should have let him follow them. They might have been nothing to do with Faith disappearing, but we didn't know now. We'd come all the way up here and when we were finally maybe getting somewhere, I'd bottled it. If something horrible was happening to Faith, maybe that would have been our chance to stop it, and instead I'd just been pathetic.

When Jake came out, I heard him stand looking at me. 'Oh, Angharad,' he said gently, squatting down beside me.

I looked up at him. He looked all blurry. He sat down next to me. 'I'm sorry for shouting at you, Angh. You're just a kid and I was a dick.'

It took me a few seconds to stop crying to talk. 'I'm sorry, Jake. I shouldn't have stopped you. I was so scared.'

He stood back up and loped to the bathroom. I heard him pulling at the toilet roll and when he came back he gave me a bundle. I tried to blow my nose as attractively as possible. 'See?' he grinned, sitting back next to me. 'I'm good at looking after crying girlies.'

I sniffed at him. I felt better, knowing that he wasn't still angry. 'Only because you make them cry.'

He smiled back, 'I don't mean to, Angh. I didn't mean to make you cry. You were probably right, anyway, I'd have probably got my head kicked in.'

He looked at me, very sincerely. 'I'm a lover, not a fighter.'

I ignored the butterflies in my stomach and pushed him. He winked at me. 'I don't even know why we're looking for that nutter. She's probably having a great old time doing some crazy shit.'

I let my head rest against his shoulder. He'd taken his jacket off. For someone so unhygienic, he smelt very clean. Like washing powder and aftershave. It made me wonder about something. 'Do you still live with your mam?'

He shrugged, rubbed my hair. 'She would be gutted if I moved out.'

'What's your brother like?'

'Why are girls always so interested in my brother? He's a dick.'

I could hear the hurt in his voice. Decided not to ask any more. Poor Jake. He tipped his head over so it was resting on top of mine. 'Angh, how do girls get such soft hair?'

I felt him tug a chunk of hair, gently. 'I get that shampoo is how it smells so good, but how does it go all silky?'

I didn't move my head. 'Are you chatting me up, Jake?'

I smiled, thinking about how much I'd have wanted Jake to be saying stuff like this a few weeks ago. If someone had told me before the steam rally that a few weeks later I'd be sitting in a hotel in Worcester with Jake Morgan telling me I had silky hair I'd probably have thought that'd be all my dreams come true. His voice sounded like a smile too. 'It's just habit, Angh, don't read anything into it.' He stopped and I felt my heart speed up. 'Unless you want to?'

My whole body seemed to be panicking. Jake was running his fingers through my hair. This was all my dreams coming true and I wished I could just relax and enjoy it. I felt Jake shift next to me, turning his body towards me. I didn't move. I tried not to think about how disgusting the carpet might be. He put his rough fingers on my chin and turned my head towards him. I closed my eyes so I didn't have to look at his face. I kept reminding myself again and again that I wanted this. Hoped my body would remember that it was having a nice time. 'Are you okay, bach?'

I waited for my voice to work. 'I feel really bad. Like I might be sick. And my head hurts.'

He peered at me, then pursed his mouth, like my mum when she's checked my temperature. 'Have you got a hangover coming?'

'I'm not hungover!'

'Come on, ' he said, and helped me onto the big double bed. 'Lie there, shut your eyes, and I'll wake you up in an hour. You're such a kid, I keep forgetting.'

'I'm older than Ella,' I said.

'That's different. And it's not a competition.'

I was pretty sure that it was. I lay back and shut my eyes but that seemed to make the room spin around above my head so I opened them again. Drinking wasn't as much fun as some people made it look.

Jake was sitting on the chair looking at his phone. When I looked at him, he put his phone down and grinned across at me. 'Everything spinning? Teach you a lesson. Good thing I came back, or God knows what you'd have been doing. I've got to call Ella in a bit, but do you want me to tell you about Phil's first? Like a bedtime story?'

I was going to nod but felt too sick. He started anyway. 'Okay, so I just called Phil, told him who I was and said Marie had given me his number when I was trying to find Faith. We had a bit of a chat and he was in town, so we met up.'

I tried to nod again, waiting for the useful bit. 'He seems like a pretty sound bloke. Mentioned Faith, said she was a bit of a handful. I told him he didn't know the half of it. So, yeah, it must be something to do with those blokes from Spoons, cos Phil didn't seem to know anything.'

Brilliant. I shut my eyes, and concentrated hard on not throwing up. I felt the bed sag when he sat down next to me.

Faith

I sat and watched a bloke pushing a toddler on the swing. I kept finding myself fiddling with the knife in my pocket. It was only small, but it had a rough side for cutting into the meat and a smooth, worn wooden handle. I kept rubbing at whatever was smeared on the blade. I started thinking. Thinking about what had happened and why it might have happened. I'd got caught up in something grim. Something where girls like me left their homes and maybe never came back.

I watched the black clouds moving over the city. You could feel that the rain was coming, feel it in the air. There was a roll of thunder, a loud one.

The dad scooped his kid up, under his arm, laughing and joking, as if they were playing a game, and ran across the field with it. I watched them drive away. The rain was splashing down on the mud in big lumps.

Jamie

I should have thought about Paul earlier. By the time we got to him, it was too late. He said Faith was looking good, which wasn't the helpful information we needed. I tried to explain that we were worried about her and that she had just disappeared from the nice job we had lined up for her. Paul kept nodding, but I'm not sure how much was going in.

There was a bar maid too. She was looking a bit shifty, like she knew something. I should have started with her, because while I was talking to Paul, I heard her gasping. Brad had got his knife out and she was bleeding. 'Fuck's sakes, Brad!'

'Sorry, mate.'

There seemed to be a lot of blood, but it didn't look like it had gone too deep. So I passed her a bar cloth to try and stop the bleeding and then we had to leg it. Brad kept apologising, but even he had to admit that it hadn't been ideal.

Angharad

When I woke up, there were drops of rain on the window. I sat up, and looked out. I couldn't see any blue sky at all. Jake was sitting beside me watching TV and texting. I wondered who, but I knew that asking would just piss him off. 'It's raining,' I said.

He winked, distractedly. I phoned my parents and tried to sound like I was having a great old giggly time with Faith. So much of a great time that I was going to stay another night. My mum wanted to believe me. I promised I'd be home tomorrow. I looked at Jake when I said that and he nodded. Once I'd finished on the phone we sat silently together. 'Last night, then, Angh. We'll give it one more go tonight, and then home tomorrow. If it doesn't happen tonight then it never will.'

I wasn't sure if he was talking about us or Faith, but I nodded. I didn't know which I wanted him to be talking about. He was so gorgeous. And so cool. And basically the whole of Llanyfenni fancied him. And everyone knew him, and if you were Jake's girlfriend then everyone would know you. And that felt kind of safe, whatever my parents would say. And screw them anyway. They weren't exactly the best judges of character. Jake was definitely less creepy than Mr Thomas, and they thought he was literally God's gift.

Then I thought about Faith. I didn't know where we were going to look and I didn't see we stood any chance of finding her. We'd tried being like detectives and failed. I was starting to think she had just disappeared. Fallen away, somewhere that people like me couldn't go. I imagined a grate, and Faith just falling through between the bars. Like a lamb that had got on the wrong side of the fence and couldn't get back. I wished I could remember her face.

I thought the only thing left to try was walking the streets. Looking in cars. Peering through windows. But Jake had a better idea. 'If those blokes are with her, we can head where they were going. Down by the canal. If you don't freak out again.'

I nodded. I thought I was past freaking out now. I just wanted to get the next few hours over with. I wanted to go home and have a bath. I wanted to fancy Jake like a normal teenage girl. And I wanted to tell my dad. I didn't care what he thought of Jake any more, and surely as soon as the police knew they would find her and she'd be safe. I didn't let myself think about all the quad bikes they'd failed to find, or the JCB. It would be Worcester police looking. Proper city police, that knew what they were doing. That cared about lost girls. I imagined lots of them, sweeping across the city, maybe with helicopters, scooping Faith up wherever she was and bringing her safely home. But just in case, I'd follow Jake to the canal and we'd have one last try tonight.

We had been walking for about forty minutes when we found Journey's End. The canal seemed different in the rain. Darker and even more abandoned. My thighs were sore from rubbing against my wet jeans. I hadn't brought a coat, so it wasn't long before I was soaked through. Jake was wearing his leather jacket. Even wet he still looked like some kind of model. Maybe even more like one. After the row of little sweet barges, there was some massive old wreck of a boat, all rusty and dark. There was a creak, like something from a horror film, and a door opened. Someone came out, holding their arm over their head to keep the rain off. They leapt down onto the path, and marched off, away from us. I hadn't seen his face properly, but there was something about the way he walked. I looked up, and there was the name of the boat painted on to some old sign that might have been nice once. Journey's End.

I grabbed Jake by the arm and pointed. 'Awesome,' Jake said and used his arms to pull himself up onto the boat. This felt wrong. I looked up at him. 'Be careful.'

He wasn't listening. He was balancing on the edge of the boat, looking pleased with himself. 'There's no one here,' Jake grinned down at me. 'Come on,' he said, reaching an arm down.

'I can do it by myself,' I said, like a toddler.

I stood on the path, looking up at the metal sides, all rusty, rain running down them and splashing loudly into the canal. I definitely did not want to climb up there. I thought of Faith. I thought about Cerys, telling me to look for Faith, and telling me that Faith was a good girl. I didn't like Cerys, but I didn't want to disappoint her either. I put my hands on the top and pulled myself up. 'Well done,' said Jake.

I looked around. My body was slow and tense. There was rain dripping off my eyebrows and stinging my eyes. 'That was one of the guys from the station,' I said.

'No!' Jake looked enchanted. 'That was a bad guy?'

'Where's the other one?'

I didn't feel like Jake was taking this seriously enough. You could tell that he wasn't the one who'd been followed round Worcester. I wondered what it would take for Jake to actually realise when he was in danger. He was peering in the window. 'Fucking hell, Angh, this is amazing.'

I didn't look. I was too busy watching. If one man was walking away, where was the other one? Jake wasn't paying me any attention. 'It's like some proper dealer's pad, like you'd see on telly. But it's very dirty. Why is it so dirty?'

He sounded disappointed, like the dealers had let him down. I kept watching. It felt like one of us should. It was properly raining, pouring down. I breathed in the funny smell you get when it rains like that. Jake was walking along the deck, towards the door. 'There's a padlock on the door, a really big one. I reckon I could smash it though, if I had the right tools.'

'Jake, where's the other guy?'

'I'm going to look around the other side.'

'Don't slip.'

Jake clambered right over the roof, and the boat rocked. I held on to a rail on the roof and waited for the rocking to stop. I wondered if you could get sea sick on a canal. I was definitely feeling queasy, but that could just as easily have been because I was so scared. I wondered if anyone had ever just stopped breathing from fear. Jake's running commentary drifted over, 'Bloody hell, Angh, they've got a proper sound system in a boat! And there's a kitchen!'

Someone came walking down the towpath, short shorts and a t-shirt and a massive sun hat, rain dripping off it. They looked at me disapprovingly. I decided that I would rather be with Jake on the hidden side of the boat, than all alone next to the path, looking like I might be about to vandalise it.

I clambered around, slowly, holding tight to the handrail. Jake had his face pressed against another window. 'There's a kettle and a tiny oven and everything! This is so cool. And a cupboard with another big lock, that's probably where they keep the drugs! They're proper dealers, Angharad! Like the ones who get kids to run the drugs for them, and make the girls do whatever they say and wear masks!'

Jake finally looked at me and his eyes were shining. 'Maybe they just wear masks on the telly. They listen to drill. You probably don't know about drill.'

I wondered if Jake was actually listening to anything he said. 'Kids like me, to move the drugs, Jake?'

The rain on the water and the metal was so loud that it was hard to hear him reply. 'Obviously not like you, girlie! Kids with families that don't care, loser kids that aren't in school, that kind of thing. No one would think that you'd be able to sell drugs. No offence, Angharad.'

'Like Faith? Kids like Faith?'

I held the railing with both hands, while black spots danced in front of my eyes.

Faith

I'm not the hysterical type, but it was becoming clear that I had nothing good in my life. Sitting on a swing, in a dirty summer dress in the pouring rain might be quite cool on Instagram, but it was cold and shit and depressing actually doing it.

Usually you can get by, day to day, by just being happy with the stuff you have, enjoying the sun on your skin and the sheep and the butterflies and all that crap. Making a big deal out of one girl and one kiss because it's the only bit of life that feels nice and right. You might wake up and think 'fuck, fuck, fuck,' but then you just get on with the day. But it was getting hard to ignore that my life was lacking some pretty important stuff. Parents, for one. Decent friends.

If Phil and Jed were happy to hand me over, then I couldn't trust anyone. I couldn't live on the odd bag of prawn cocktail crisps forever. I wasn't going to see my dad again. It was easier to leave him out of my life than to be like my mum, waiting for him to be someone different.

If I was Angharad, I thought, I'd go to the police. Or phone my mum. And if I was Angharad, none of this would have been my fault. I wouldn't have been selling weed, I wouldn't have been handed around like a pass-the-parcel prize. I know how the world works. The police aren't there for people like me.

Angharad

Jake had his arms around me. 'Angharad?'

I opened my eyes. All I could see was his jacket, water streaking down it. He was stroking my back. 'I've got you,' he said happily.

'Jake –' my voice was croaky.

'You're safe, I've got you.'

I pushed his arms away. 'I'm worried about Faith.'

I explained to him, carefully, that if these guys were drug dealers, like the county lines drug dealers on TV, that Faith was exactly the kind of person they showed getting hurt. He looked at me dubiously. 'But not in Llanyfenni, Angh. And Faith's sorted. She's not the sort of person they're talking about. She doesn't need looking after. She just needs fetching back to town.'

I couldn't be bothered to keep explaining to him. 'We need to find her,' I said.

'We will, don't worry,' Jake said reassuringly.

He didn't understand at all.

Faith

I couldn't stop thinking about Daria. Lying dribbling on the settee, sure that all she had to do was just one little thing and then everything would be alright. I was angry with myself because I knew that I couldn't just leave her with them. I had to try and help her. Maybe I wasn't a bad person after all. Which was inconvenient. I didn't want to go and help her. I wasn't brave enough or strong enough or clever enough. I wondered where Angharad had got to.

Angharad

There were a few minutes where I thought everything might be alright. We might bang on a window and Faith might be inside, or we might hear her shouting. I sat on the roof watching for people coming towards us, while Jake crashed about, banging on windows and shouting. We couldn't get inside, and that was scary too. Faith might be trapped inside, or unconscious. 'Do they make the kids take drugs too?' I asked Jake.

He stopped crashing about and laughed. 'No one needs to be made to take drugs, Angh. If Faith is helping out these guys she probably gets stuff for free.'

'What sort of stuff?'

'Anything she wants, probably.' Jake stared down into the canal, sounding envious. 'She can probably try anything for free, so that she can recommend it. Like bike stuff, they give it to me for free and then when someone asks me what boots I'm wearing or whatever, I tell them. I'm like a walking advert. They watch me, and want to be like me. And that's called sponsorship. Faith probably gets to do the same thing.'

I wished I was with someone else. Even Cerys, for example, wouldn't be so annoying. Even Ella. Jake was still explaining things to me. 'You've got to stop thinking that Faith's not having a good time. She's probably never had so much fun. Just because you didn't like those guys, and because you wouldn't want to be partying with strangers –'

I had to stop listening again. Jake seriously seemed to be implying that I'd just somehow got off on the wrong foot with the white t-shirt men, rather than that they had nearly attacked me for trying to talk to Faith. 'But don't worry,' he continued, 'I'll take care of them for you. I'll get Faith back for you.'

He was standing, looking up at me on the roof. 'Don't worry,' he said again. 'I'll find her.'

Faith

I walked back towards the bridge near the flat. I knew this was probably a bad idea. But I couldn't imagine anything else I could do. I wanted it to be over and I knew I had to get Daria out of there. Maybe she would listen, now. So I just kept walking. Everything felt weird. Like I was watching myself in a film. I looked very small. It felt like there should be music playing. Something dramatic. And I really wanted a drink. Or maybe a hug from that nice bar maid.

Angharad

We kept walking, until we ended up back on the bridge where I had thought Jake might kiss me when we bought pizza. He stopped there, looking down at me. 'Do you think in an alternative universe somewhere, we got it together?'

He sounded sad. 'Jake, I'm sorry.'

'No worries. Maybe when you're older.'

But somehow, now, that didn't seem likely.

Faith

I hoped that while I was walking, I would have some time to think of a great way to get Daria out of the flat. Including a way to get Daria to understand that Jamie was even worse than his aura seemed. But it turned out there was no time for that at all.

I was standing under the bridge, hiding from the lashing rain and then there was Jamie and his ratty little face, heading towards me. I was so fucking hungry and tired that I thought I was losing it, but it was definitely him. He wasn't wearing a coat. His hair was slicked down across his forehead. He didn't see me at first. I stood up, straight. I felt my fingers wrap around the warm wood on the knife. I wished I'd thought harder about how this was going to work. It wasn't too late to run. I glanced behind me and there was another shape coming towards me. Maybe a passer-by, wanting to help but I thought probably not. I felt myself freezing and swore at myself quietly to get moving. My body wasn't listening. There was nowhere to run now, just a wall up on one side of me and the water on the other.

'Faith,' Brad said from behind me, as if he was delighted to find me.

I didn't look back. If I had to stab someone, I knew who I was starting with. I stepped forwards, out into the rain, towards Jamie.

Angharad

I didn't recognise Faith at first. I was looking down at her wondering why anyone would be walking around in a summer dress in this weather, even as I felt rain trickling down my stomach under my t-shirt. Then I saw the man walking towards her, and I knew straight away that the something bad was happening. 'Jake!'

We both realised it was Faith at the same time. 'Stay here!' Jake said and took off down the steep slope to the canal. As he ran off I realised there was another man, walking behind Faith. I hoped she knew he was there. They were all moving so slowly, Faith walking away from the bridge towards the boats and the men all walking towards her, like she was reeling them in. She looked very small and very alone.

I started to chase after Jake and then thought of something that might help more. 'Oi!' I shouted loudly.

The men looked up, and Jake arrived behind the guy walking on his own and punched him. For a minute I thought Jake was going to save the day and defeat the evil baddies. He was even stronger than I had expected. The man's head seemed to snap forwards and he staggered sideways. But then he turned round and he and Jake were grappling with each other on the path.

I ran down to the canal bank. The path was muddy, and I felt my feet skidding a bit underneath me. Now I was stuck behind Jake and the man and the rain was falling too fast. I couldn't see Faith at all. Not good. And then suddenly there was a massive splash and Jake and the man were in the water and I could see Faith, behind them.

I felt ridiculously awkward for a second at seeing her, as if we were just on the street in Llanyfenni. Then I realised one of the white t-shirt men were trying to push her up the path, away from me, back towards some boats. 'Oi!' I shouted again, thinking surely someone would hear me, even through the noise of the rain on the water.

I glanced back to see what was happening to Jake even though I had no idea what I was supposed to do to help. They both seemed to be standing in the water, near the edge, still gripping each other and doing a lot of pushing and pulling, waist deep in water.

I turned back to Faith. She was being hustled down the path backwards, kicking and biting. I ran at the man, but without knowing what I was going to do next. Faith stopped biting for a split second and stared at me. He yanked her arm up behind her back and I could see the pain on her face. And I stopped worrying about it being awkward and stared back. I still didn't say anything in case I embarrassed myself. And she grinned at me, all happy, like a pirate about to attack a ship. I grinned back. And then her face went twisted and white.

Faith

Jamie pulled my arm up even harder behind my back. Everything already hurt so much I wouldn't have thought it could get worse, but it did. I wondered how much pain someone could be in before they just passed out. Suspected I was close.

I was so fed up with being hurt. I guess Jamie was probably a bit fed up with me too. And he had nothing to lose. He just kept walking back, holding my arm up high, and I just had to keep going with him. He was hissing in my ear, 'You like this, bitch?'

I couldn't talk. He kept hissing. 'Your girlfriend is coming. Think she wants to come with us?'

I tried to bite him. He pushed his arm back into my mouth till my jaw felt like it was going to be pushed right off. My tongue was pushed against his skin and my mouth filled with saliva. And Angharad did nothing. I tried to push him sideways but he was like a brick wall.

And then he stepped back onto one of the metal rings the boats were tied to. He barely tripped but Angharad suddenly looked like she'd woken up. She leapt across to one of the little boats and grabbed a flower pot. She had the flowers and everything. She picked it right up, and lobbed it straight at him. It must have hit him because his arm went slack in my mouth. And I pulled the knife out of my pocket and jabbed up behind me. I was aiming at his eyes. I don't think it actually went in far. That's what I've been telling myself since, anyway.

Angharad

I wasn't expecting the flower pot to have much effect, but Faith said later that he'd already had a bit of a battering on his head and she was stabbing him so I guess having a flower pot hit you in the head was enough. And then Faith wriggled free and the bloke had mud and earth all over his face and his white t-shirt. Faith grabbed a long pole from the boat and waved it around. She swung it low enough that the guy tripped and staggered back. Faith was bending over him and for a moment I thought she was helping him. Until I saw the blood.

Then she was beside me, grabbing my hand. 'Quick,' she said, and I followed her obediently. For a split second we stood on the edge of the canal, then she grinned at me again, let go of my hand and dived into the water. I followed her before I even thought about it.

I'm a pretty good swimmer, and I dived shallow, but the canal was full of crap. We were lucky. Really lucky. I kicked something with my foot but kept my eyes tight closed, and my mouth and swam as fast and as far as I could. I stopped when I crashed into the opposite bank. Even with my lips squeezed shut, I could taste canal.

Faith was already there, holding the metal edge of the canal with one hand. Even though I'd thought no one was ever going to pay any attention to me shouting, people were leaning over the bridge. I could see some were starting to head down the side of the bridge, running but cautiously, not sure what they were getting into.

The guy was out of the canal, and they were both standing staring across at us. One of them was holding the side of his face. I wasn't sure what they'd do but when they saw the people heading for them they started to back off, then turned and ran. Jake seemed to still be stuck in the mud.

I thought we should probably go and help him, and I

turned my head to say something to Faith, but she had already pulled herself up and onto the bank, and was reaching down to help me up. For a minute we struggled like that, then I let go and got up by myself.

Water was pouring off me. I sat up beside Faith. She was watching the small crowd on the opposite bank.

The scary men had gone, and Jake seemed to be trying to explain that he had been helping some girls, not just fighting. No one was looking for us yet, so I guess they didn't believe him. I realised Faith was holding something in her hand. She held it out to show me. It was a steak knife. I took it from her and dropped it in the canal. I felt Faith take my hand, and leant my shoulder against hers.

I had no idea what we were going to tell people and how we would avoid talking to the police now, or how I was going to get back home without my parents finding out any of this had happened, but I suspected it would all be alright, one way or another. I looked up and even though Worcester was full of lights, I could still see the stars high above us.

Angharad

'We need to get Daria,' Faith said.

We were still sitting, leaning against each other like tired soldiers. 'I met Daria,' I told her.

I felt her nodding. 'I heard.'

'Where is she?'

'Some shitty flat up there.'

She waved vaguely. I didn't move. It was a warm night, but I was starting to shiver. I didn't want to find Daria. I wanted to sit with Faith, and then go and have a cup of tea and a nice hot shower. I might even have sugar in the tea. 'I don't want to,' I told her.

She was nodding again. 'Me neither.'

We sat for another minute, watching the rain. 'Come on, then,' she said, getting up.

'What about Jake?'

We looked across at Jake, who seemed to be showing a woman in a tight dress a cut on his muscular stomach. It was hard to see through the rain, but she was definitely standing very close to him. 'Maybe she's short-sighted,' Faith said, rolling her eyes.

She looked down at me. 'Do you fancy him?'

I felt myself blushing. Not because it was true, but because I could see now what a pathetic, embarrassing thing it was to have ever fancied Jake Morgan. 'A bit. By accident.'

She laughed, her mouth wide, as if she couldn't even imagine being self conscious. 'We should probably take him with us. He could charm Daria.'

'Will she need charming?'

I couldn't imagine wanting to stay in a flat with those horrible men. Faith screwed up her mouth. 'She might. She thinks she owes them money and she's kind and gullible. She won't want to let them down.'

'What if she won't come?'

'We can't leave her there. They aren't very nice.'

Faith looked away, back across the canal. I wanted to ask her what had happened, but I was scared. She reached down, and I took her hand and stood up. We stood in the rain. Every bit of me was soaked with horrible canal water and rain was dripping off my eyebrows into my eyes.

I wanted to kiss Faith again, just to see. It felt a bit uncaring though, when Daria might be in real trouble. Faith was watching me, smiling. She reached up and touched my cheek. 'Thank you,' she said.

I shrugged, awkwardly. The time before Worcester seemed a long time ago. It was impossible to remember when coming here was a choice. I knew I wasn't exactly the hero though. 'It was Jake really,' I said.

'Huh. Right. We better go.'

We stood, looking at each other. My breath was stuck in my throat and my chest felt tight.

Faith

Angharad was standing in front of me, shivering a bit. Her t-shirt was plastered over her wet skin. It had gone see through. I tried not to look. Looked anyway. Looked back up, into her beautiful eyes. I felt myself smiling more, I couldn't help it. She was smiling, a bit, too. I knew we needed to go. The thought of Daria, alone in the flat, with Jamie and Brad all pumped up and furious, made me feel sick. But for the first time in days, I felt safe. I knew it wasn't sensible.

She moved closer. 'We need to go,' I said, not moving.

I realised I was a cliche, now, a bad film. She smiled properly, like she was thinking that too. 'I'm scared,' she said.

'I'll look after you,' I said, far too sincerely.

She laughed. I turned across the canal and looked at Jake again.

He was a muppet, but I guess at least he had kept Brad busy splashing about. And it was nice of him to have come, even if it was only to find his cheap drug supplier, or come onto Angharad, or probably both.

Thought about Angharad being fooled by him pretending to be nice. Thought about them, coming to Worcester, together, like they were a team and I was some loser needing rescued. 'Fuck it,' I said. 'Let's just leave him. Daria's too old for him anyway.'

She looked shocked, and then she laughed. 'I'm so glad I found you.'

She sounded embarrassingly sincere too. I could feel myself grinning, like everything was magically going to be okay because she was with me.

Angharad

Faith pulled me up the canal bank. There was one of those big chain link fences at the top and we went along it until we found a gap in the wire. I could feel my wet jeans rubbing against my thighs again. I hoped we weren't going to have to move too fast. I'm not really a sporty sort of person. I hoped Faith realised this.

But Faith let go of my hand and started running. I did my best to chase after her. I should have known she'd be the running type. I had thought we'd head back over the bridge, but Faith ran the other way, along a back street. There were street lights, but no people. I knew I was already panting. I followed Faith onto a main road, and across another bridge, and then down another back street. My lungs hurt more with every breath, and my thighs stung, and my skin felt hot. I imagined I was steaming in the drizzling rain. The flats we stopped outside were modern and shining. Some of the flats had balconies and pot plants and fairy lights, like something you'd get in Cardiff or London. They were the coolest flats I'd ever seen. I looked at Faith. 'Here?'

I must have sounded dubious, because she rolled her eyes at me. 'You think people can't be in shiny flats and sell drugs? How do you think people get rich, Angharad?'

I wasn't going to be patronised by someone who couldn't even say my name. 'All sorts of ways, Faith. There's all sorts of ways people can make money without breaking the law!'

I knew I sounded like my dad. But Faith didn't seem to be listening. She was heading for the modern, shiny door, waving the keys at it. I trailed after her, and she turned around to face me. Suddenly I was kissing her again, and I didn't care about her English accent or her criminal behaviour. I just wanted to be close to her, and touching her.

Faith

I knew this wasn't what we needed to be doing right now, but I wasn't going to be the one to stop it. I leaned back against the door, let her kiss me. Let myself just think about her warm mouth and the way she was pushing herself against me. I pushed my fingers into her soft, wet hair, pulled her in. Closed my eyes, and tipped my head back, and felt her lips on my cheek, and my neck. Then she stopped.

Angharad

I stopped kissing her when I remembered Daria and that the white t-shirt men might appear any minute and hurt me. I looked at Faith. It wasn't awkward. It wasn't awkward at all. She was smiling at me, looking shy and different. 'I'm sorry I ran off. Before.'

I couldn't help smiling back. I took her hand. 'Come on,' I said and she put the key into the lock.

The outside door was heavy. We walked slowly up the stairs. I didn't know what Faith was feeling, but I was terrified. Every step I kept thinking that I wouldn't be able to go any further. 'One more step,' I kept telling myself. 'Just one more step.'

Faith

I was scared. I'd finally got away from the baddies and got the girl – or maybe she'd got me – and now I was going back, as if I wanted just one more chance to be mixed up in all their stuff. Didn't let myself think of all the lovely things that I could be doing with Angharad. I opened the door at the top of stairs. The corridor stretched in front of us, long and shiny and empty.

I pushed open the door of the flat slowly. I was too scared to move any faster. I could feel Angharad's hot breath on my arm. I'm not usually a fan of being panted on, but for some reason Angharad's panting was reassuring. We waited while the door swung open.

I was ready to run, but nothing scary happened. There was no sign of Brad, or Jamie. I took a step inside.

Angharad

The flat was empty. You could tell as soon as you got inside. And it was amazing. It was like something on an Ikea advert, all shiny metal and stuff that people had chosen and not just had left to them by their nan. 'Wow.'

Faith looked at me, her mouth twisted. 'Yeah.'

'Is this where you were? When I was looking for you?'

Faith nodded. 'Yeah.'

I took her hand. She led me through the flat. She shrugged. 'Dim Daria.'

I couldn't believe we'd been so brave for nothing. And that Faith was speaking Welsh. She shrugged. 'Jake taught me.'

'Where is she? What's happened to her?'

Her eyes had gone weird, like when someone's trying not to show they're crying. 'Let's get out of here.'

We walked back out of the flat and into the rain. We took the keys and left the door open. I don't know why. I didn't look at Faith, in case she was the kind of person who didn't like being looked at while she was crying. I kept hold of her hand though. I was thinking. It was definitely turning out that real life was a lot more complicated than chess or Skyrim, but one of the things with chess and online gaming is not giving up. 'What about that boat?'

Faith

I had been so sure that we were going to find Daria at the flat. I had been psyched for a fight, and Daria being a pain and needing shouting at and Angharad probably not doing much but still being there. I leaned back on the shiny smooth flat wall. Rain was pouring down from a balcony edge and down my back. It didn't matter. I couldn't exactly get wetter. I tipped my head back. Didn't let myself think about Daria's beautiful face, Daria's pathetic belief that Brad and Jamie were on her side, that everything was going to be okay. Daria's pathetic belief in Phil. Didn't think about Olly. Didn't think about how I had thought Brad at least was on my side. I breathed in. 'Okay. Let's go.'

We ran through the rain, my flip flops slipping on the wet paving. Still holding hands, as if that would keep us safe. It was downhill to the canal, and we skidded onto the towpath and stopped. Part of me had thought that the boat would be gone, but it was sitting there looking as black and ugly as before. From up here, I could see the steel door, sitting wide open in the rain.

A barge came through the bridge, making a chugging noise like it was a train. We stood silently, watching it pass. The rain had stopped, suddenly, like it had started. Everything had that smell, like it does in summer when it rains. There was no one on the towpath, except a figure, tall and slim, striding through the mud. Fucking Jake. I almost felt pleased to see him.

Angharad

Jake started running when he saw us. 'Girlies!'

Then he stopped dead, staring at us. 'What's up?'

Faith waved at the boat. 'We need to go in and check if anyone's inside.'

Jake was filthy. And when he got near, he smelt like the canal water but worse. But he clambered back up on to the deck and went in the door. I could hear him making excited noises. Faith and I looked at each other then she swung herself up and followed him in.

Faith

The kitchen door was open too, and the money was gone and the coke and there was no sign of Daria. We went back outside. 'What now?' I asked.

Jake's phone wasn't working after he'd been in the canal but he was confident it would once it dried. Angharad's was missing altogether. Angharad had said firmly that we needed to tell her dad. I thought I'd be pissed off at her, bossing us about, but it was just a relief. I was so sick of being in charge.

I watched her stop talking, and think for a minute, like her brain was a little computer working out calculations and what ifs and reaching dead end after dead end, but just starting again anyway. Jake opened his big mouth to interrupt and I kicked him. He looked at me like he was a little puppy and I was some cruel owner, but at least he didn't say anything. Angharad snapped back into gear. 'I need to talk to my dad. We need to find a phone. We'll go back to the White Horse.'

Jake winked at me. 'OK, babe. Whatever you want.'

I ignored him and started walking. I was pretty sure Jake had nothing to add to the conversation right now.

Angharad

I thought if I could talk to my dad the horrible feeling of wrongness would go away. I knew he couldn't be angry with Faith, that he would understand. I realised I wasn't that fussed about him being angry with Jake. I knew that we probably should phone the Worcester police but I was just too scared. And I didn't see that the police would find Daria that night anyway.

Faith

Jake had managed to insert himself between Angharad and I, and was banging on about his fight. 'So Mel — that hot old woman — said —'

Mel had looked about thirty to me, but I guess if you were used to manipulating fifteen year olds into having sex with you that she might seem old. Jake didn't seem to care that no one was replying. 'She said that she couldn't believe it when I just leapt into the water after him —'

I thought about making him shut up again, but it felt rude after he'd sort of rescued me earlier. Even if I knew his motives were showing off and trying to sleep with Angharad, I still felt that I owed him. Ironic, because usually the more you shout at men the more they think that you have a special relationship. Usually I shouted at Jake a lot, and he was more and more grateful when I actually sold him some weed, but right now I just couldn't be bothered. 'Mel thought it was pretty amazing that I was so strong, but I told her I was nothing special, it was only because I rode stunt bikes.'

Even if I wasn't going to shout at Jake, I still couldn't bring myself to encourage him. We walked up over the bridge and through the busy streets. Swimming in canals and stabbing people felt unreal, or like it had happened a long time ago. I wondered when it would be time to sleep. I knew I was crying and crying, because I was safe and Daria wasn't.

People were looking at us weirdly, all three of us wet and filthy and Angharad with her torn t-shirt. When Jake took a break from telling us how brave he was, he took his jacket off and put it round her.

Angharad

Our room key was still in Jake's jacket. We snuck back in through the front door trying to look inconspicuous. The owner of The White Horse was standing behind the desk in the hallway and drinking a bottle of red wine without bothering with a glass. She seemed unsurprised by an extra visitor and the fact that we were all soaking wet and Jake was covered in mud. Jake gave her his special charming grin and hustled us both into the bedroom. As soon as the door shut, he went straight into the bathroom and slammed the door. 'Dry the phone and call your dad, then,' he shouted through the door.

We stood there and listened to him stamping about and then the shower turned on. Faith was shivering. 'You need to take those wet clothes off,' I told her.

She just looked at me, with her huge eyes. 'I can't,' she said forlornly.

I went behind her and unzipped her dress. Her shoulders felt cold when I touched them. I peeled her wet dress off her as if she was a toddler, and she stepped out of it. I took one of the blankets from the beds and helped her wrap it round her shoulders. She sat on the bed. I took the phone out of Jake's coat pocket and lay it on the bed, hoping for the best. I tried the on button, just in case, and surprisingly, the light came on.

Predictably, my Dad was fuming and pretending not to be. He asked gentle questions like, 'So you went to Worcester with Jake Morgan?' and 'So Faith has been selling drugs in our town?' When I got to Daria though, things changed. Presumably it was obvious to my Dad that Daria's disappearance was all the fault of our toxic society and the government.

When he asked where I was, I realised that I didn't want to tell him. I just wanted to cry. I was cold and wet and tired and my dad was far more interested in Daria than me. This was probably a dream for him. An inner city kid, led astray by drug dealers and only my dad able to see that she was the real victim. 'In a hotel. Jake is paying.'

Luckily thinking about Jake distracted my dad again. 'That Morgan boy! Swanning around town like he's a gift from God.'

I imagined Jake, all shining gold, delivered by God. It was a shame that Jake wasn't what I'd hoped. Or maybe not, given that I was in a hotel room with him and Faith together. I wondered if threesomes happened in real life or if it was just the kind of thing teenagers told each other.

When I tuned in again, my dad was still banging on about Jake. 'And you! You need to be more careful Angharad, and make better choices. You should know better. And now, the three of you are there, in some fancy hotel –' I looked around at the weird teddy bears, staring at me – 'and that poor Daria is being used and misused by some drug dealers. You don't understand how dangerous these people can be. This is serious, Angharad, she needs help.'

'If only there was something you could do, right now,' I said, not caring if he heard the sarcasm.

'There is something I can do! And I'm going to do it!'

And he put the phone down. Faith looked at me. I rolled my eyes and shrugged. 'He's going to try.'

'They wouldn't kill her,' Faith said, in a quiet voice.

'I don't think so. I don't see why they would kill anyone.'

She had stopped crying, but her face was white and she seemed smaller and defeated. As soon as Jake came striding out of the bathroom, a towel wrapped around his waist, I took Faith's hands and led her into the bathroom. There wasn't really space for the two of us and the blanket but I hung it on the window handle and hoped it wouldn't slip off. The floor was wet and Jake seemed to have used the only towel. I reached past Faith and turned the shower on and she stood obediently underneath the warm water.

I left her in the shower and went to see if there was a kettle. Jake was standing staring at his reflection in the window. I made Faith tea, with all the sugar, and handed it to her in the shower. She held it in both her hands and drank it slowly with the shower water all falling in it, then handed it back. She beckoned at me, smiling a bit. 'Coming in?'

'No,' I said firmly.

She sighed, made a sad face, and stepped out of the shower. I put the blanket back around her shoulders. 'You can wear my pyjamas,' I told her. 'In my bag. Shoo.'

I hoped Jake would manage not to be a dick for five minutes while I was in the shower. When I stuck my head out the bathroom door, Faith handed me the blanket. It was funny seeing her in my pyjamas. I had a sudden flashback of how she'd looked the first time I met her, with her long brown legs and her tiny dress. I put on yesterday's dirty clothes, which were all I had left. Jake put the TV on and Faith and I sat side by side on the bed. My hair was wet but I felt warm. Faith's hand reached for mine. She felt warmer now. I put the blanket back around her, and she tipped slowly sideways and shut her eyes. 'Thank you,' she said, not looking at me.

'It was Jake too,' I reminded her, but I didn't think she'd heard me.

Jake put the TV on and then filled the kettle back up, and made us both another cup of tea. 'There's no fucking sugar left.'

Faith's head was on my knee. I held my cup carefully so I didn't wake her up, and Jake sat up in the other bed and we sat and drank tea and watched shit late night television. After a bit, Jake looked across at me. 'Angh, I don't want you to feel that you need to hold back on some big romantic reunion or anything. Just because I'm here. You know, you can just pretend I'm not. Do whatever you want, you don't need to feel uncomfortable. I just want you to know I'm fine with it.'

He nodded very sincerely at me, and then added meaningfully, 'Anything, Angharad. Whatever you feel. You two just carry on.'

We both looked at Faith, crashed out on the bed next to me. I rolled my eyes at him, but I was too tired to be worrying about Jake being a big pervert. Faith's head felt heavy, her hair trailed across my blanket and my pyjama bottoms rucked up on her brown legs. It seemed too good to be true that we were all safe together in this freaky hotel, soft toys staring up at me from the floor. I grinned across at Jake and he grinned back. 'Fucking wild,' he said, nodding happily.

He turned back to the TV and we sat and watched some dodgy film with vampires and women buried alive in coffins.

Marie

Cerys had been popping around most days. That day she brought a ginger cake. My favourite. She made it herself. Cerys said that it's probably best not to have a stranger in the house, even if she is a friend of Faith's. We prayed together for strength, and then we swept the kitchen floor. Well, I swept and Cerys put the kettle on.

Jamie

There's no point looking down your nose at me. Or thinking that I'm scum. I mean, what the fuck is a girl like Daria
going to do? When you're imagining her perfect future, if
she hadn't got mixed up with me, what does it look like?

Angharad

When I woke up it was morning and Jake's phone was ringing from somewhere in my bed. It took me a minute to find it. I had managed to get all tangled up in Faith in the night. I got my arm and head free and hung off the bed to reach it. Jake had opened an eye to watch. I guess he was worried about his phone or optimistic about boobs falling out in the disentangling.

My parents were demanding to know exactly where we were so that they could come and rescue us. They were on the edge of the city already. I was gutted. I wasn't ready for them at all. We all got up and then sat around not saying anything.

They arrived fuming about the White Horse and then when I managed to bundle them into our room without the owner seeing them they took one look at Jake, and fumed even more. It would have been a good idea if Jake had put a top on, I guess.

It was all pretty awkward, with my dad glaring at Jake and Jake looking more and more shifty and saying less and less. I kept telling my parents that he had been really kind to me and had paid for everything, but that just made them more suspicious. Faith didn't have anything to change into, so she was just standing there in my pyjamas glaring at everyone out of sleepy eyes like a tiny, furious owl.

I tried to hug Jake goodbye but it was like hugging a concrete pillar. I didn't want to leave him. He was lecherous and annoying but at least he didn't seem to think everything was Faith's fault. I was crying again by the time we got to my parents' car. My dad had his police coat in the boot and tried to give it to Faith, but she shook her head.

Faith and I sat in the back seats and my parents tried to pretend that they didn't think I was insensitive to poor Daria's plight (my dad) or just generally unchristian (my mum). I thought Faith might get angry and explain where she'd been and what had happened to her, but she just turned and looked out the window like none of us were there.

Angharad

It turned out that Jake was right. Dan Davies came out to talk to Faith. Told her to stay out of trouble and wasn't interested in Daria. It was Cerys who kept coming to see my dad again and again and read laws and articles and rules about young people and drugs to him. It turned out she used to be a lawyer. Which seemed unlikely, because surely lawyers would be more interesting, but I was the only one who seemed dubious. Then my dad decided that Faith was a victim of society too, and he was going to be the one to explain that to our police. And suddenly, it was all fine, and everyone thought Faith was brave and amazing. Everyone except Dan Davies and Mr Thomas, anyway.

Mr Thomas

Thou art weighed in the balances, and art found wanting. A biblical verse particularly applicable to Marie, I think. A reminder that we are answerable to God for our actions and inactions. I might preach on it and hope that she takes it into consideration when deciding whether her daughter should be dressing more appropriately in church.

Angharad

It seemed a little bit unfair that my Dad was really, really cross with me. It's not like I hadn't been trying my best to do the right thing. I tried not to feel that it wasn't fair that no one even shouted at Faith about the knife. She got sent to talk to lots of nice ladies and given tea and biscuits – all different kinds, she told me smugly. It took a while before she told them everything, but I'm not sure telling them really made much difference. When the police found the flat, there was no one there and they didn't seem to be able to trace the tenant. I don't know why and my dad wasn't saying. He had gone from saying loudly that he wouldn't rest until Daria was found, to saying that sometimes good people can't stop bad things happening. The last Faith heard, Phil and Jed had been questioned and no one could find Brad or Jamie or Daria, or if they could then they weren't telling. If those were even their real names, I guess. And Journey's End had disappeared too. I don't see how a boat can disappear, but no-one else seems to think it's important.

The only person who didn't seem cross with me was Cerys. She was too busy being cross with Mr Thomas for being an interfering fool with no Christian charity. She says Marie needs all the help she can get, and a Christian who won't help someone in need is no Christian at all. She went with Marie to the GP and she doesn't talk about what happened there, but Marie seems happier and someone comes round once a week to help her keep the house tidy, which saves Faith doing it.

Cerys also tells everyone loudly that Faith is a lovely young girl and she just wishes young girls had been allowed to court whoever they wanted in her day and they would have all been a lot happier. I suspect Mr Thomas only puts up with this because he's still thinking about Cerys's money and the church roof fund. So maybe he is a true Christian, sacrificing himself for the good of the roof. Cerys told Faith that she is leaving all her money to a charity who help teenage addicts recover and, anyway, a lot of it has gone to pay a private detective in Worcester try and find Daria. Cerys says that the detective says that he is confident that he's getting closer, but then he would say that.

Sam stopped coming to church. His mum said he had left the Christian Gaming group and was playing with a team from Coventry and getting paid for it. Paid quite a lot, she said, nodding at me, like she had a point to prove. He'd had an interview with some Formula One people and they had offered him an apprenticeship, so he was off to somewhere down near London in September. When I saw him in town, Ella was hanging off his arm pouting up at him. I guess he didn't dislike all types of physical contact after all. He stopped when he saw me, and carefully said hello. Ella grinned happily. She seemed to have forgotten she hated me, or maybe I was supposed to be jealous. 'Hi, Angharad,' she said.

I smiled at her, just to show that I wasn't. 'Hi, how's it going?'

I was asking Sam, really, but it was Ella who answered, 'We're going to buy me a dress. Sam has a big prize thing and he's invited me! It's quite a big deal, actually.'

She sounded delighted and did a quick pirouette just to show off. Smug cow. Sam smiled awkwardly, and she led him away. I watched for a minute, feeling a bit like Sam might need rescuing. Then I saw his hand slide down to her bum, and figured he was just fine.

Jake's still around. I thought we'd hang out, the three of us, but it didn't really happen like that. A few days after we got back, my dad and I went into town and we saw him with a girl. Young and blond. I guess she was probably about fifteen. I waved at him and he winked but we didn't talk or anything. The girl was giggling and flicking her hair. Just the way girls are with Jake, but my dad just started fuming again, and then we had to go and find the girl's mum in the shop where she worked so my dad could have a word with her. It was completely embarrassing. And it's not like Jake's a paedo. Paedophiles are old and scabby and Jake's young and beautiful. I don't get why my dad doesn't see that.

After my dad went and had a word with Jake it was all a bit awkward. I kept telling my dad that Jake was the one who said we needed to find Faith, and if it wasn't for him she'd probably be with Jamie and Brad still and anything could have been happening to her. It felt really wrong that no-one understood that. My dad just pursed his mouth up and told me to stay away from either of the Morgan brothers. So Jake was right about literally everything, and the shit did hit the fan as far as me and him went.

Faith went back to school. She didn't like it, but she went anyway. She said she didn't have any friends and everyone stared at her and talked about her and every now and again she got taken out of class and had to sit in a room with some hippy to see if she wanted to share her feelings. She was supposed to be sitting GCSEs but everyone knew she was going to fail them. She didn't care; she had a college place all sorted, she was going to study agriculture. 'So I can fit in with all you Welshies,' she told me, rolling her eyes.

Her dad never did try to find her or come back to be Marie's knight in shining armour, and Faith hasn't seen him since that pub in Worcester. She seems fairly cheery about that.

I stopped going to church too. I could see my mum and dad loved it and it was really important to them, but I wanted to take some time and think about whether it was important to me or not. I thought maybe, if I knew I wasn't just going for the sake of it, I might quite fancy going back. That's what I told my mum and dad, anyway. I haven't decided if it's true. And I spoke to my parents about my studying. Or the way I wasn't actually studying. They were shocked and cross at first that I'd been doing nothing for the last year, but I'm pretty sure we all knew it wasn't exactly my responsibility.

After a lot of huffing and puffing my dad has cut down the hours he works so he can be a bit more use at helping me. And once I'm sixteen, I can go to college anyway. I've been looking at courses. To be honest, I'm not sure that maths and physics are my thing, but some of the other courses look good.

I don't know what I want to do with my life or anything yet. Sara – the other home educated girl – carried on not being a complete bitch. It's not like we were friends, but we smile at each other now and say hello, and I think one day soon I'm going to ask if she fancies going to the cinema. It's not like I'll die if she says no, and I reckon she might say yes.

And Faith and I… well, it's complicated. We don't talk much about what happened, but she did talk to a journalist from our paper about it. She missed out big bits of the story, but she did say that she'd been selling drugs and she wasn't any more and she said a lot about Jake being the one who was worried and had gone to find her. My hero, the headline was. Jake hasn't said anything, but there's a photo of the paper on his Instagram feed. She says that when she told the police about Phil and Jed, she knew that she'd never be able to go back to Worcester. Neither of them have even texted her to see if she's okay, but maybe you can't blame them.

I'm still getting to know Faith and she's not who I thought she was. I think about her when I wake up – sometimes because my phone's buzzing away to say that she's texted. She comes round every few days and we sit on my bed and watch Gossip Girl and Jane the Virgin. I showed her how to play chess and she showed me how to roll a cigarette and the best way to do cartwheels. We go for long walks up into the hills when she's not at school. She's got waterproofs now and wellies and all the normal sorts of stuff. She looks like everyone else here, and so do I.

Epilogue

Faith

No surprise – Llanyfenni is weird at Christmas. Someone brought a sad Christmas tree to the square, and it sat there for a week looking a bit lopsided before they put some lights on it. Multi-coloured lights, like it was 2002. There was carol singing in the square. With the town choir. I was embarrassed for them. Then embarrassed for myself when I cried when they sang. Mum cried too, so I gave her a push to stop her. On the other side of her, Cerys put an arm through hers. Next to me, Sue stood stoutly, singing loudly. I smiled at her, and when she smiled back, I took her hand. She let me, then squeezed it, and we held hands all through the rest of the singing. On the other side of the square, Angharad was standing with her parents. I expected Angharad would be singing along devoutly, and she was, but she was also watching me.

It's been hard, not fancying Angharad, but it seemed the right thing to do. We were both lonely, and it would probably just turn into a mess. What with me being an exploited victim of gang-related activity and sometimes a bit of a bitch, and her being so weird and judgemental. My counsellor made very disapproving noises when I mentioned dating Angharad, but that could be because she's a homophobic arsehole.

Aside from that, Angharad was the only friend I had. I didn't want to mess that up. So we'd had three months of casual, cheerful texting and walking and I tried not to think about her in every spare second. I thought it was probably okay to be a bit dishonest with her, if I was being dishonest with myself too. And I was waiting for her to say something, or to argue with me. But she didn't. And then Sara came along and started inviting her to things, and then suddenly she did have friends. Including one who patently fancied her. This wasn't what I had planned. I hadn't been fretting too much – there were a lot of hot, theoretically heterosexual girls in school to get to know – but I missed Angharad.

But standing watching her in the glow of the horrible lights, I felt the certainty that we should just be friends drain out of me. I didn't want to just be friends. I wanted to touch her soft, round cheeks and stroke her soft hair. I wanted to hold her hand. I wanted to tell people she was my girlfriend. I sighed. I was new to this thinking long-term thing. It was hard.

Angharad

Faith came to find me when everyone was leaving the square. My parents struggled not to look disapproving, but I waved at them, smiling reassuringly, and turned my back on them.

Faith's face was flushed with the cold. She didn't have a hat. We stood under a streetlight, staring at each other. The skin around her lips was blue. Things that I had tried to stop thinking about were flooding my brain. Ideas about her skin, and her mouth and her tongue. I couldn't speak. Maybe I didn't know how any more.

There were people moving past us – heading home, or to the pub. I could tell they were grumbling as they moved round us, but I still didn't move, and neither did she. She was smiling, and I was too. And then suddenly the street was empty, and we were alone. She stepped towards me, and reached a hand towards my waist.

'Faith –' My voice sounded embarrassingly hoarse, as if I had a sore throat. I could feel my heart thumping, as if it might just burst out through my ribs.

Her hand was on my embarrassing jeans, her fingers hooking though the loops pulling me closer. I could feel her breath on my face. 'Angharad,' she said, her voice so soft I could hardly hear it. 'I –'

She smelt of chocolate. I took a step towards her. There were millimetres between us. My arms dangled beside me, until I realised I could just put them around her. I felt her body pressing against mine. Her cold hand slid underneath my jumper and her nails scraped against my skin. I took a deep breath. 'Faith, I really like you, and I'm bored of just being friends.'

I could feel her laugh even through all my layers. 'Me too.'

We stood, wrapped together under the streetlight. Outside a pub, some men whooped. Maybe at us. I slid my hands up into her hair. Even her hair was cold, like she'd come out before it dried properly and it'd started to freeze. Like the ice queen. I bent to kiss her. Her lips melted against mine. In another place it might have started snowing, but this is Mid Wales. The rain was bitter. 'Should we go inside?' I asked, but she grinned and shook her head.

'Kiss me properly,' she said.

So I did.

The End

About the Author
JJ Lambert

Joanna Lambert lives in Carmarthenshire with her improbably wonderful wife and children. She studied Creative Writing at Aberystwyth University and is currently trying to persuade them to supervise research into Twm Siôn Catti. She has been published by The New York Times, Gwyllion Magazine, Lucent Dreaming and The Cardiff Review, amongst others and is a part of Queer Writers Cardiff. She home educated her children, though claims no credit for the way they have turned out.